"Then you'll admit I'm not a child?"

Domine challenged him, her lips still warm from his kiss.

"No," James muttered savagely. "You're not a child. And if it pleases you, you have the power to infuriate me into actions I would otherwise believe myself incapable of. But it won't happen again."

Domine's heart sank, and out of the bitterness in her soul she taunted him, "How can you be sure? You think you can plan your life so emotionlessly—maybe you can't."

He laughed. "What kind of emotions are you talking about?"

"How about...love?" she murmured quietly.

"Love?" There was a cruel glint in his eyes. "What's that? I admit I don't know, and I doubt if you do, either."

But I do, Domine thought desperately. *I know too well....*

ANNE MATHER

storm in a rain barrel

Originally published as Harlequin Presents #14

Harlequin Books

TORONTO • LONDON • LOS ANGELES • AMSTERDAM
SYDNEY • HAMBURG • PARIS • STOCKHOLM • ATHENS • TOKYO

Harlequin Presents edition published July 1973
ISBN 0-373-15013-X

Second printing July 1973
Third printing August 1973
Fourth printing November 1973
Fifth printing July 1974
Sixth printing August 1974
Seventh printing April 1976
Eighth printing September 1976
Ninth printing February 1977
Tenth printing March 1977
Eleventh printing March 1979

This *Harlequin Presents Collection* edition published March 1981

Original hardcover edition published in 1971
by Mills & Boon Limited

CHAPTER ONE

THE rain fell in a steady downpour, causing rivulets of water to run continually down the window, obliterating, if only momentarily, the dripping trees and sodden grass. The sky was dark and heavy, and every now and then a low rumble of thunder echoed round the heavens accompanied by a flicker of lightning which lit up the prematurely darkened room. There was a high wall all round the garden outside and Domine wondered why its presence, which had previously suggested the environs of a prison to her, should now represent all that was secure and familiar.

Why didn't he come? she asked herself again. What could possibly have delayed him?

She moved from her seat by the window and walked restlessly about the room, hugging herself as though to ward off the sense of apprehension that assailed her. She glanced at the small wrist watch she wore. Was it really only a little after three-thirty? It seemed much more than two hours since lunch was over. If only it wasn't so dark and dismal, maybe she might have felt better. As it was, the weather had added its own sense of gloom to an already gloomy occasion.

She returned to her seat by the window, pressing her nose against the pane, breathing a misty circle, and then drawing on it with an idle finger in the way she had often been chastised for doing. Impatiently, she rubbed out the clown's face she had etched, and heaved a sigh.

How much longer was she going to have to wait?

Reaching for her handbag, she rummaged about in

the bottom and came out with the packet of cigarettes which had been hidden there. It was strange to realize that after today no one would care whether she smoked or not. She grimaced. Unless James Mannering objected to girls smoking, of course. She quelled the sense of panic that rose within her, and hastily brought out a box of matches and lit the cigarette she had already placed between her lips. Drawing on it deeply, she removed it from her mouth with unsteady fingers and replaced the burned-out match in the box. It would not do, even now, for Sister Theresa to find her with cigarettes. The habits of nine years die hard.

She looked out of the window again. From here the sweep of the gardens could be seen, and away to the right, if she pressed her face against the pane she could glimpse the drive that led up to the main entrance of the Convent of the Holy Sisters.

Her sense of nervous tension intensified as the powerful roar of a car's engine could be heard on the road outside the convent walls, but the sound eventually died away and she realized that whoever had been driving the car had swept on by, past the closed gates at the foot of the drive.

She shivered. Surely she would not have to wait much longer. Didn't James Mannering realize how upset and disturbed she was bound to be? Did he imagine she would take the news of her altered circumstances impassively, without having the imagination to speculate on what would happen now?

She rose to her feet again and going across to the empty grate stubbed out her cigarette and put the stub inside the box of matches and replaced the box at the bottom of her handbag. Then she looked at herself in the tiny mirror attached to her compact. Mirrors were not in plentiful supply in the convent and the reflection she saw in the powdered glass was not very clear. What would James Mannering think of her? she thought dully. And what might she think of him? What could you think of a man you had never even met? Someone who had summarily been given responsibility for you?

She pushed back the untidy fringe of chestnut hair that strayed across her wide brow. She could see nothing of beauty in olive-tanned skin, and large brown eyes. Her brows and lashes were dark, which she supposed was an advantage, particularly as the only make-up the girls were allowed to use was powder and lipstick, and that in very small quantities. Her hair was long and thick, and rather silky when she brushed it thoroughly, but as it had always been confined in one rather chunky braid she had never had much chance to appreciate it.

Sighing, she put the compact away and began to compose what she could say to James Mannering when he arrived. It was difficult to decide with any certainty how she would treat him, she knew so little about him. Of course, as he had been a contemporary of her father's, he must be over forty, and his work, as a playwright, was not encouraging. He was probably terribly sophisticated and 'with-it' and would use all those awful exaggerated adjectives she had heard artists use at the local coffee-bar whenever she and one or two of her friends had gone alone into town on special occasions like someone's birthday. She supposed he was a kind of uncle really, except that they were not related by any blood tie. Why, *why* had Great-Uncle Henry done it? What had he hoped to achieve? After all these years – refusing to acknowledge him as his son, and then finally making him his heir!

She shook her head. Not that she cared about the

money, particularly, except that had she been six months older everything would have been so much easier. She would have been eighteen then, and capable of refusing anyone's charity.

As it was, she had had no choice but to fall in with the terms of her great-uncle's will. She had not attended his funeral, but that had not surprised her. After all, in all the years that she had been in his care, she had never once visited Grey Witches, the house her great-uncle owned in Yorkshire, and where he lived for nine months of the year. The other three months he devoted to Domine, and during those times they visited a hotel in Bognor which had become Domine's only home away from the convent. There they had spent every Easter, summer and Christmas holiday for the last nine years.

She cupped her chin on her hands, wondering what would have happened to her nine years ago, had Great-Uncle Henry not stepped in. She could still remember the horror of the train crash which had killed her parents, still recall the screeching of the brakes, the groaning of the overturning carriages, the shrieking of the women, and the cries of the children. She shivered again. Oh, yes, she still got nightmares about that time and the awful impact it had made on her life.

Then, Great-Uncle Henry had been a deliverer, taking the eight-year-old Domine away from the loneliness and misery of the orphanage and installing her in the comparative comfort and pleasant surroundings of the Convent of the Holy Sisters. Not that Great-Uncle Henry had been a religious man, he had not; but he respected the church and all it stood for, and as he affirmed that he could not possibly have Domine with him all the time, they spent these holidays together. Soon now, Domine had been hoping to leave the convent and go on to college, or maybe even university. She was bright and intelligent, and the sisters had been confident she would do well. But all that had been changed by the sudden death of her great-uncle. He had been her father's uncle, the husband of her grandmother's sister, and therefore his interest in Domine had been all the more admirable as their relationship had only been by marriage. But he had had no children of his own, or so he had said, and he had given Domine the kind of moral background she needed, had given a stay to her existence. But now—

She started, almost guiltily, as the door opened and Sister Theresa stood there regarding her compassionately. 'Well, Domine?' she said, with a smile. 'Are you ready?'

Domine's eyes widened. 'You mean – he's here!' Her heart fluttered wildly.

'Yes, Mr. Mannering has arrived,' replied Sister Theresa. 'I believe he had some difficulty locating the convent in this driving rain. And after all, these roads are not very well signposted, are they?'

Domine shook her head. 'I – I didn't hear the car,' she stammered.

'Didn't you? Well, perhaps the storm disguised its arrival. Or maybe you were not thinking about it,' she murmured gently.

Domine swallowed hard. In truth, she had been so wrapped up in her own thoughts she had not been conscious of her surroundings. Nodding, she lifted her handbag and smoothed the skirt of the pleated pinafore dress she was wearing over a white shirt blouse. She felt young and gauche, and wished she had something a little more inspiring to wear. But perhaps it was as well that she had not. Any attempt at sophistication on her part would appear quite ludicrous.

9

She followed Sister Theresa's flowing-robed figure along the stark tiled corridor and down a flight of stairs to the ground floor. Here a beautifully carved statue of the Mother and Child gave warmth to an otherwise bare hallway. The glowing colours of their robes and the gilding of their headdresses brought their cold features to life, and Domine twisted her fingers together nervously. She was not a Catholic, and until now she had felt apart from their religion, but suddenly its strength enfolded her.

Sister Theresa knocked at the door of the study where the Reverend Mother awaited them, and ushered Domine into the room. She entered rather tentatively, her eyes going immediately to the figure of the man who stood motionless beside Reverend Mother's desk. He had his back to the door as she entered, and was staring out of the window that surveyed the same view that previously Domine had been contemplating. The rain had not eased at all, and lamps had been lit in the study to relieve the gloom.

The man turned as Sister Theresa closed the door, and looked piercingly at Domine with eyes that were a strange light shade of blue. Cold eyes, they were, she thought palpitatingly, and could see no warmth in his face. He was not a handsome man, his features were harsh and darkly tanned, lines deeply etched beside a mouth which had a sensual curve. He was, she supposed, a little under six feet in height, with broad shoulders but an otherwise lean body. His hair was very dark and straight, and sideburns grew low on his cheeks. She couldn't begin to guess at his age, although he was younger than she had vaguely imagined, certainly younger than her father would have been had he lived. And certainly he was not the artistic aesthete of her imaginings. He dressed like a business man in a dark suit with a matching waistcoat, and wore a thick dark car-coat overall. At the moment, his coat was unfastened, and his hands were thrust deep into the pockets of his overcoat. Raindrops glistened on his dark hair, and Domine reflected that he had not wasted any time discussing her with Reverend Mother. She wondered what Reverend Mother thought of him, and gathered from the old woman's expression that she was still rather doubtful about delivering her charge into this man's hands.

However, she appeared to disguise her thoughts, for she rose as Domine approached her desk, and said: 'Ah, there you are, my child. As you can see, Mr. Mannering has at last arrived to take you home.'

Home? The word stuck in Domine's throat. Where was home now? Some place belonging to this man? The hotel in Bognor? Or Grey Witches, finally?

'Yes,' she faltered now. 'How – how do you do?' Awkwardly she held out her hand, and with an imperceptible shrug James Mannering shook hands with her. His hands were the only artistic thing about him, she thought, long and lean, with smooth, rounded nails.

'Hello, Domine,' he said dispassionately. 'Are you ready to leave?'

'Oh, but—' began Reverend Mother, glancing at Domine and then back at James Mannering. 'I mean – won't you stay and have tea with us? It – it would give Domine a chance to get to know you. After all, you are a complete stranger to her, are you not?'

James Mannering compressed his lips for a moment. 'Yes, we are strangers, Reverend Mother,' he agreed, 'however, I don't believe we could possibly begin to get to know one another with a third party present.' His gaze flickered almost sardonically. 'Besides, as you know, I was delayed in arriving because of the weather and I should prefer to return to London before dinner time.'

Domine felt an awful tightening of her stomach muscles. Until this moment she had been so concerned with meeting the man himself that she had not fully realized what being his ward would mean. She would be subject to his desires in everything, and wherever he said she should go she would go. She shivered, and Reverend Mother intercepted her nervousness. With a stiffening of her shoulders she said:

'Nevertheless, Mr. Mannering, I must insist that you have tea with us. As you are a stranger to all of us, I should like to discuss Domine's future with you. It is natural that we should want to know what your plans for her are, and what arrangements have been made for her to continue with her studies. Domine has always been one of our most intelligent pupils, and it would be a shame if she were to waste her talents – now.'

James Mannering drew out a cigar case and glanced at Reverend Mother rather shrewdly before extracting a cigar and placing it between his teeth. 'Very well,' he said laconically. 'Very well, by all means have tea. But I'll just have this' – he indicated the cigar – 'if you don't mind?'

The question was unnecessary, Domine felt sure. James Mannering was the kind of man who would respond to few restrictions. She had the feeling he would smoke his cigar whatever Reverend Mother might say.

Reverend Mother bit her lower lip rather sharply, and walking to the door she opened it and called: 'Sister Theresa! May we have the trolley now, please?'

Domine hovered in the centre of the carpet aware that James Mannering's eyes lingered on her rather speculatively, and she wondered how on earth she would ever get used to being his ward. Even six months seemed to stretch endlessly ahead of her. Mannering responded to a suggestion from Reverend Mother that he should sit down, and lounged into a deep leather chair by the window while Domine perched on the edge of a high-backed chair which was placed beside the desk. Sister Theresa wheeled in a tea trolley containing cakes and sandwiches, and Domine was forced to accept a sandwich and nibbled it without enthusiasm. The grimness of the day seemed to have intensified a hundredfold, and she could hardly believe all this was actually happening. There was an air of unreality about the whole affair, and for the first time she pondered the man's reactions to being landed with a teenage ward without a real knowledge of the world outside the convent walls. During the past few minutes she had become aware of her own ignorance of life in general, and a feeling of despair gripped her. If she had been the kind of girl who sometimes came to the convent, girls like Susan Johnson, one of her friends, she would have felt able to cope, but Susan had a normal home and background, with two elder brothers to have fun with, to share experiences with, while Domine had had no one for the past nine years but a rather elderly gentleman whose ideas of entertaining the young were confined to trips to the cinema or the theatre, and occasionally a visit to some charity function. She had listened to the other girls gossiping about clothes and pop-records and boy-friends, but apart from this she had no knowledge of their world.

Reverend Mother began to question James Mannering about his plans for Domine, but his replies were non-committal and after a while the old woman seemed to realize she would learn little this way.

Instead, she turned her attention to Domine and said:

'Have you made any plans yet, Domine? Have you thought about what kind of occupation you might find?'

Domine hesitated, conscious of Mannering's interested attention. 'Obviously, it's a little early for me to have made any plans,' she began awkwardly, 'however, at the end of the six months – when Mr. Mannering's responsibility towards me ceases – I expect I shan't find it too difficult to take up some kind of office work. My examination results were good, and I have the qualifications for bank or library work if I need it.'

Mannering leant forward, studying the glowing tip of his cigar. 'Oh, come on now,' he said, in a harsh tone, 'this isn't an auction market, Reverend Mother. It isn't necessary for Domine to sell herself to me. She's been handed to me – on a plate, so to speak, and you need have no qualms that her future won't be adequately attended to!'

Reverend Mother looked flabbergasted by his plain speaking, and Domine's pale cheeks turned scarlet at his tone. 'I wasn't aware that Domine was attempting to sell herself to you in any way, Mr. Mannering,' the elderly nun said tautly. 'We are simple people here, with simple beliefs, and possibly a misguidedly simple attitude towards the world outside, but nevertheless, we are aware that for a girl of Domine's age to obtain a suitable position she requires the necessary qualifications.'

Mannering looked up, those light blue eyes glacier clear. 'And what do you consider a "suitable" position?' he questioned sardonically.

Reverend Mother's cheeks coloured a little. 'I do not feel that I should be forced to answer your questions, Mr. Mannering,' she replied, sharply. 'But, as you ask, any of the positions Domine has mentioned seem perfectly acceptable to me.'

James Mannering shook his head. 'In effect you are ruling out any occupation that might fall short of your rigid set of values,' he said, bluntly. 'If Domine is well qualified, she may prefer a job in something a little more inspiring than an office or a bank, or a library either, for that matter. There's advertising, for example. Or the arts. Or even something as devastating as the theatre!'

'Obviously, we are speaking at cross purposes, Mr. Mannering,' said Reverend Mother, sniffing a little. 'Am I to understand that Domine is to be thrust into the theatre because that is your world?'

'Hell, no!' Mannering got to his feet. 'I agree, we are talking at cross-purposes. However, I don't see that it matters, for a while at least. Domine won't immediately be taking up any kind of occupation.'

Domine glanced at him. 'Why?'

Mannering shrugged. 'We'll see,' he said, dismissing her question. He fastened his overcoat and went on: 'I don't think we're achieving anything by discussing it here and now. It's too early to make any assessments.' He looked at Reverend Mother. 'I'll keep you in touch with Domine's movements, if that's what you would like. And now, as time is fleeting, and as I said I want to be back in London before dinner, perhaps you'll excuse us?'

Reverend Mother had no choice but to agree, and she sent Domine to collect her things and to say goodbye to her friends. Susan Johnson was waiting in Domine's room on her return, and her eyes were wide and excited.

'I say, Dom,' she exclaimed at once. 'Is that gorgeous male really your James Mannering?'

Domine gave her a weary glance. 'What gorgeous male?'

'Heavens! Don't tell me you haven't noticed!' gasped Susan. 'Jane and I saw him arrive. We were downstairs in the hall when he came in. Is it James Mannering?'

'Yes.' Domine stuffed the rest of her toilet articles into an overnight case, and lifted it together with the larger case that contained all her belongings.

Susan shook her 'head. 'Well, I must say you don't look very pleased about it,' she exclaimed rather impatiently. 'Surely he's not at all like you had imagined.'

Domine glanced in her direction as she walked towards the door. 'Well, I'd agree with you there,' she said dryly. 'Honestly, Susan, I know absolutely nothing about him. I don't even know where I'm going to live!'

Some of her trepidation showed in her voice and Susan approached her sympathetically. 'You know he's quite a well-known playwright,' she pointed out thoughtfully. 'And after all, you're not old enough to arouse any – well, other kind of interest in him, are you? I mean – I don't want to be unkind, Domine, but you are rather naïve, aren't you? Me!' She laughed. 'I'd give anything to be in your shoes! Being ward to a famous man like him! Having the opportunity to meet all kinds of exciting people! Not just to marry the first man that asks you because you think his prospects are good!'

Domine half-smiled. 'You will write to me, won't you? I'll let you have the address as soon as I know where it is.'

Susan nodded vigorously. 'Of course. After all, you might invite me to come and stay some time.'

Domine sighed, and then walked slowly along the corridor towards the stairs again. As she began the downward descent, she saw James Mannering waiting in the hall with Reverend Mother, and when he saw her struggling with the cases he left off speaking to the nun and mounted the stairs lithely to take them from her. Domine, unused to any kind of assistance with her belongings, glanced at him in surprise, and saw a faintly mocking glint in his eyes as though he had been glad to escape from Reverend Mother's catechism.

Sister Theresa joined her superior to say good-bye to their charge and the double doors of the convent were opened to admit a blast of chilling air, accompanied by driving rain. Domine, who had donned her school coat, a navy gaberdine, pulled up the collar, while James Mannering said: 'Wait here!' peremptorily, before dashing out into the storm.

A few moments later, the roar of a powerful engine heralded the arrival of his car, which he drew up close to the entrance so that Domine had only to cross the terrace and climb into its warmth and luxury. She said good-bye to Sister Theresa, and then to Reverend Mother, and biting back a choking feeling in her throat, she ran and climbed into the limousine. She saw, through the pouring rain, that James Mannering had returned to say good-bye to the nuns, before striding back to the vehicle and sliding in beside her. The engine had been running and he thrust it smoothly into gear and raised one hand in farewell as they began their journey.

Domine lay back in her seat feeling overwhelmingly shaky now that she had left all that was familiar behind her, and for a few minutes she stared blankly out at the awful weather and thought she would never experience a storm without remembering this afternoon. James

17

Mannering did not speak to her at once, giving her time to collect herself, and manoeuvring the sleek car out of the gates and along the rain-washed country roads. The Convent of the Holy Sisters was situated about five miles from Guildford, and it wasn't until they reached the main road to London that her companion glanced her way.

'Well?' he said, somewhat wryly. 'Are you going to cry? Or will you save that for tonight – in bed?'

Domine stared at him in astonishment. She was unused to his blunt manner of speaking, and endeavouring to assume a little of his candour, she replied: 'No, I shan't cry now, Mr. Mannering. As for tonight, I don't even know where I'm to spend tonight!' She compressed her lips to prevent them from trembling.

Mannering gave her a lazy stare. 'Don't you? Didn't the solicitor explain the situation to you?'

'I haven't seen the solicitor,' replied Domine tightly.

Mannering frowned. 'Is that so? You mean it was all done by correspondence?'

'Of course. Besides, what could the solicitor have told me? From the tone of his letter, he seemed as surprised as me!'

Mannering's frown deepened. 'Now why were you surprised, Domine? Did you expect to be Henry's heiress?'

Domine clenched her fists. 'I think you're most objectionable, Mr. Mannering!' she exclaimed. 'I didn't imagine anything. Great-Uncle Henry wasn't old – at least, not that old. When I was eighteen I expected to go to college, and afterwards – well, I suppose I just thought I'd get a job and find somewhere of my own to live.'

Mannering gave her a wry glance. 'Okay, I'll accept

18

that,' he nodded. 'I'm sorry if I'm riding you, kid. Perhaps I'm so used to the rat-race I've forgotten there are still mice around.'

Domine flushed. 'You still haven't answered my question. Where am I to stay? Where am I to live?'

Mannering drew out his cigar case and lit a cigar before replying. Then he said: 'Tonight, you'll stay at my apartment – in London. Tomorrow we'll drive up to Yorkshire.'

'To Grey Witches?' exclaimed Domine, in surprise.

'Sure, to Grey Witches!' He frowned. 'I don't intend to sell the place, you know. What's the matter? Doesn't that appeal to you?'

Domine shook her head. 'I didn't think about that either,' she murmured, wondering with a sense of excitement whether Grey Witches was to be her home. It would be wonderful to have a real home after all these years.

Mannering gave an exasperated shrug, and then they encountered a stream of traffic entering London and for a time his attention was focused on negotiating a series of traffic lights. Domine looked about her with interest. She had never really visited London. When she was younger, living with her parents in Nottingham, it had never appealed to her, and afterwards Great-Uncle Henry had avoided it like the plague. 'Nasty, unhealthy place,' he had called it, and Domine had been too inexperienced to offer an opinion.

James Mannering's apartment was the penthouse of a block of luxury dwellings, and once inside the air-conditioned environs of the lift Domine forgot the vile weather outside. The lift swept upwards smoothly, and then whined to a halt at the thirtieth floor. They stepped out on to a pile carpeted corridor that led to double doors into his apartment, and Mannering went ahead of her, using a key to admit them.

Immediately a suave little man appeared from the direction of what she later learned to be the kitchen, and Mannering introduced him as Graham while he removed his overcoat.

Domine smiled, and shook hands, and Mannering said: 'Graham is a gentleman's gentleman. He was employed by Lord Bestingcot years ago, but he's been with me for about ten years now, haven't you, Graham? He's endeavouring to instil the attributes of a gentleman into rough clay like myself!' He smiled, and Domine was surprised at the change it brought to his harsh fatures. She was begining to see why Susan had thought him attractive. There was something particularly masculine about him, and his hardness, she thought, would appeal to some women.

Graham took Domine's gaberdine, and suggested they might like some coffee, but after ascertaining that dinner would be ready in about fifteen minutes, James Mannering waved him away.

'We'll have something a little more appetizing,' he remarked, and nodding, Graham went to attend to the meal. Then Mannering looked at Domine, standing hoveringly by the door. In truth, she was still recovering from the impact the apartment had made on her, with its plate-glass windows, giving a panoramic view of the city, and the soft carpet underfoot into which her feet sank. There were deep red leather chairs, and occasional tables made of ebony, while in the alcoves, fitted shelves supported books, hi-fi equipment, and a super-luxury television set. The room was lit by tall standard lamps designed in sprays, while the heating was concealed but comfortable. And despite its artistic design, the room was the kind of place where one could relax without worrying too much about ultra-tidiness. Just now, a pile of manuscript lay on a side table, while some magazines were strewn on a low couch. It had a lived-in air, and Domine wondered whether Great-Uncle Henry had ever been here.

'Come and sit down,' invited James Mannering, indicating the couch. 'Take your shoes off; make yourself at home. If you're to be my ward for the next six months, we might as well get used to one another.'

Domine hesitated, and then she stepped forward, and did as he suggested, subsiding on to a couch that was softer than anything she had previously experienced.

'Now! What are you going to drink?' he asked, walking over to a cocktail cabinet. 'Port, sherry, Martini? Or just some fruit juice?'

Domine bit her lip. 'Fruit juice, please,' she said, folding her hands in her lap.

He glanced round at her, looked as though he was about to protest, and then seemed to change his mind. 'All right,' he agreed, and mixed her a lime and lemon. 'There you are!' He poured himself a stiff measure of whisky and swallowed it at a gulp, then he poured another before coming to sit opposite her, on a low chair, regarding her with lazy, yet intent, blue eyes.

Domine sipped her drink, and looked about her nervously, wishing he would not study her so intently. She could feel the colour sweeping up her neck and over her ears, washing her face a brilliant shade of tomato. Then he seemed to grow bored with embarrassing her this way, and said, instead:

'Haven't you any questions you want to ask?'

Domine looked down at her glass. 'Heaps,' she agreed candidly.

'Well, go on, then. Ask?'

Domine felt tongue-tied for a moment. 'Have – have you written many plays?' she asked tentatively.

Mannering lay back in his seat regarding her impatiently. 'Oh, for God's sake,' he exclaimed. 'What does that matter? Come on, Domine, stop being such a mouse for once, and speak your mind! Doesn't it bother you that Henry should have thrust you so heedlessly into my hands?'

Domine's fingers tightened round the glass. 'Of course it bothers me. In fact, I wanted to speak to you about that. It – it might be a good idea if I stayed here – in London, I mean. I could easily get a job, and I suppose there are bed-sitters and things—'

'Oh, no!' Mannering raised his eyes heavenward. Then he stared at her again. 'Oh, no, Domine, most definitely, *no*! Old Henry knew exactly what he was doing when he handed you into my care. He knew that once I'd seen you, talked with you, got to know what kind of innocent you really are, I wouldn't dare to let you out of my sight. Leave you here in London, indeed! Good God, girl, you haven't the faintest idea what could happen to you here – in *swinging* London, as they say! Oh, no! Like I said at the convent earlier, right now you're in for a holiday.'

Domine sighed. 'But I don't want to be a nuisance—'

'A nuisance?' He shook his head. 'My dear girl, you began being a nuisance three weeks ago when old Henry died. There's not a chance that you're going to stop now, and certainly not by attempting to be independent. How old are you, fifteen? Sixteen?'

'Seventeen!' retorted Domine, somewhat jerkily. 'You know that as well as I do!'

He smiled. 'Yes, well, maybe I do at that. But right now you look about fourteen, and considering the promiscuity of girls today I would place you mentally among the twelve-year-olds!'

'*Thank you!*' Domine got unsteadily to her feet. 'You needn't imagine that because you've been given my guardianship that you can speak to me as you like!' she gasped angrily. 'I may look like a child, and I may appear to be one in your sophisticated eyes, Mr. Mannering, but I'm not, and I'm not as ignorant of the way of the world as you imagine!'

He looked up at her mockingly. 'Are you not? Then forgive me!'

She turned away from his mockery then, unable to stand this verbal baiting any longer, and he seemed to repent, for he said: 'Oh, Domine, this will have to stop, you know. It's no good our arguing all the time. All right, I'll accept that you're on the verge of young womanhood, but there's a hell of a lot you've got to learn, and you won't learn it in the space of a couple of weeks.'

She looked back at him. 'I don't expect to,' she said unevenly.

He leaned forward then, studying her thoughtfully. 'And you won't get anywhere unless you start asking some questions,' he remarked. 'Like, for instance, why Henry left everything to me.'

Domine flushed. 'That's nothing to do with me,' she murmured.

'Of course it is!' Mannering shook his head, apparently amazed at her lack of curiosity. 'Look, did he never talk about me – about my mother?'

Domine shook her head uncertainly. 'Not that I can remember.'

'Did he talk about Grey Witches?'

Domine shook her head again.

'I see. And you never visited there, did you?'

23

'No.'

Mannering heaved a sigh. 'Obviously his intention was to keep both sections of his life apart. He could hardly have taken you to Grey Witches without arousing a lot of unpleasant questions – unpleasant for him, that is.'

'Why?' Domine's brows drew together.

'Because my mother lives at Grey Witches. She always has.'

'What!'

He shrugged. 'Where else would a man's housekeeper live?'

'Your mother was Great-Uncle Henry's housekeeper?' Domine stared at him. 'I – I see!'

He lay back in the chair again. 'Now, just what do you see, Domine?' he asked, sardonically.

Domine flushed. 'Well – well, that explains a little of the mystery.'

'There's no mystery,' he retorted dryly. 'Your great-uncle was a man, like other men. His wife was an invalid for many years, or maybe you didn't know that. After all, it was long before you were born. At any rate, my mother was ultimately more attractive than his virtue.'

Domine's colour deepened. 'I see,' she murmured uncomfortably.

James Mannering got impatiently to his feet. 'Oh, God,' he said exasperatedly, 'I can almost see your mind working. What kind of reading matter did you have at that establishment you've just left? Not the kind that lends itself to a situation of this kind, I'll be bound. I'm not the illegitimate son, in the legal sense of the word. My mother was married when she produced old Henry's heir!' There was mockery in his dénouement of his father's actions.

Domine bent her head. 'You didn't have to explain yourself to me.'

'Dammit,' he muttered, almost angrily now. 'I'm not attempting to explain myself to you! My father was no saint, and I'll admit when I learned of my connection with him, I hated him! That was when I was a teenager, when I was like you, beginning to find my feet — my identity, if you like. At any rate, I'd had enough of the simple life in Hollingford. I needed an excuse to escape, and that provided one. It was later, after I'd lived in London for a few years that I realized what a stupid attitude I'd adopted. Perhaps I'd realized I was human, too, by then, and humanity possesses many frailties, as you'll discover in time.'

Domine twisted her fingers together. 'Your — your mother? She's still alive?'

'Sure. Hell, she's only about sixty now. My father's dead, though, my adopted father, that is, and believe me, he was more of a father to me than old Henry could ever have been. Don't expect too much sympathy, that's all, from me regarding Henry Farriday! His ideas could never be mine!'

Domine shook her head, still slightly bewildered. 'I wonder why he never told me that you were his son,' she murmured incredulously. 'We — we even went to see a play of yours once, in Brighton.' She bit her lip, and James Mannering gave an exaggerated sigh.

'Like I said,' he murmured, 'we had nothing in common.'

Just at that moment Graham arrived to announce that dinner was served, and they walked across the lounge and through to a small dining-room with a circular polished table, and chairs upholstered in buttoned brown leather. A low light hung over the table, and illuminated the crystal glasses and sparkling silver cutlery. Domine wondered what her great-uncle's feelings had been when he discovered that his son was achieving success. Had he been pleased? Or had the knowledge soured him? The latter, from the course of his attitude in later life, seemed the most likely. Although she had been grateful to him for all he had done for her, she began to wonder what his motives had been for helping her, if indeed he had had any. Was it possible that his reasons for involving himself in her life had been anything to do with his own disappointment in not being able to acknowledge James Mannering, the playwright, as his son, as his own flesh and blood, without causing a great deal of talk and speculation, and possibly even scandal in a place like Hollingford, which she had learned from reference books and maps was not a large place? If that was so, he must have been sadly disappointed that he had died before discovering whether she was to make anything of her life. Even so, he had still kept his son in the forefront of his mind, and it was to him that he had endowed his heritage.

CHAPTER TWO

LATER that night, as Domine lay between the sheets of
the most opulent bed she had ever slept in, she re-
viewed the events of the day in detail. It had been such
a strange day, and yet she could not now admit wholly
to a feeling of unhappiness. Indeed, there was a disturbing sense of excitement running through her veins,
a feeling she had never before experienced, and which
was preventing her from falling into the dreamless
sleep she usually achieved.

She thought about the girls at the convent, wondering whether they were thinking about her. Susan would
be. Susan had seemed intensely interested in her new
situation — and her new guardian.

She rolled on to her stomach as she thought about
James Mannering. She had not known many men in
the course of her young life, and certainly no one even
vaguely resembling him. He was hard, and she suspected he could be ruthless when it came to getting
what he wanted, and yet she thought he was kind.
There had been a trace of gentleness in his manner
with her, and she had appreciated that.

During dinner he had questioned her extensively
about herself, discovering every aspect of her life at the
convent, and her subsequent holidays with Henry Farriday. She smiled as she thought that despite his as-
sertions to the contrary he was very like his father in his
single-mindedness and purposefulness. Great-Uncle
Henry had asked a lot of questions, too. He had always
been interested in her accomplishments and it was par-
tially due to his encouragement that she had done so

well at school.

After dinner was over, James Mannering had excused himself, leaving her to Graham's care. He had a business appointment, or so he said, and she had not liked to question Graham about his employer's movements. Even so, she had been disappointed when he had not returned by ten o'clock, and Graham had suggested she retire for the night. As she had not then discovered the layout of the apartment, Graham had shown her round, and she had been suitably impressed by the large rooms with their fine appointments. It was a huge place, with four bedrooms with adjoining bathrooms, as well as the lounge, dining-room and kitchen, and a compact study where Mannering worked at his typewriter. Graham occupied a self-contained bed-sitting room which adjoined the kitchen, and which had its own entrance from the corridor outside.

Domine's own room was decorated in pastel shades of blue and green, with gold curtains and bedspread, and a bathroom with taps of beaten gold. There was a shower, too, and as she had never taken a shower in her life before she used it before getting into bed. Her cotton pyjamas seemed rather utilitarian beside the cream silk sheets, but she merely shrugged and turned out the light, glad of the anonymous darkness.

Up here, high above London, there was no sound of traffic, no intruding sense of the outside world, and she thought rather sleepily that it must be something like the cabin of a jet-liner.

It must be awfully late, she thought suddenly, when there was a slight sound outside her door, and she realized someone had entered the apartment. Leaning over, she switched on the bedside lamp and looked at her watch before hastily switching the lamp off again. It was after two o'clock! She lay back on her pillows staring up at the ceiling. It was very late for anyone to be conducting a business appointment, she thought reluctantly. Obviously, that had only been an excuse to escape from her presence for a while. Perhaps he had a girl-friend, some special woman he was hoping to marry. She frowned. Somehow, since meeting him, since having him take the time to come and collect her from the convent, she had begun to think of him in rather the manner she had thought of Great-Uncle Henry. Almost as though she was important to him, just as he was important to her. How silly she was to imagine that a man like James Mannering, rich, famous, powerful, and physically attractive should consider her anything more than a child he was temporarily responsible for, and who must indeed be nothing but a nuisance to him. Indeed, hadn't he said earlier in the evening that she was just that?

With a grimace, Domine punched her soft pillow into shape and flung herself down upon it, wondering why the excitement she had felt earlier had somehow dissipated.

When she awoke, a faint filtering of light was trying to pierce its way into the room through the slats in the venetian blinds, but it was a dismal light, and from the steady beating against the windows she gathered it was still raining.

Sighing, she slid out of bed and padded to the window, pushing the slats of the blind apart and peering out. It was a grey morning, the sky still heavy and overcast, and as it was only late October she thought it was going to be a long winter if this was anything to go by. She shivered, but not with cold, the apartment was already warm and comfortable, but the apprehension she had felt the previous day had returned, and

29

she wondered whether her opinion of James Mannering would undergo any changes today.

She glanced at her watch, and gasped. It couldn't possibly be after eleven o'clock! She stared at the tiny pointers aghast. Good heavens, what would James Mannering think of her, sleeping till this hour? At the convent she would already have been up four hours!

She hastily entered her bathroom, sluiced her face and hands, cleaned her teeth, and with unsteady fingers unplaited her hair. Brushing it vigorously, she quickly re-plaited it again, and then went and dressed again in the uniform outfit she had worn the previous day. When she emerged from her bedroom, the lounge was deserted, and she looked about her doubtfully, wondering what she ought to do to attract attention to herself.

However, she was saved this anxiety, by the arrival of Graham. He was carrying a vacuum cleaner and looked rather disturbed when he saw Domine.

'Good morning, Miss Grainger,' he said, with a smile. 'I'm sorry – did the vacuum wake you up?'

Domine smiled rather tremulously in return. 'I don't think so, Mr. Graham. At any rate, if it did, I'm glad! It's terribly late! What must Mr. Mannering think of me?'

Graham shook his head. 'First of all, my name's Graham, just Graham, there's no need for formalities,' he said kindly. 'As to the other – well, Mr. Mannering himself told me to let you sleep on. He said you would probably be tired. Overwrought, perhaps.'

Domine sighed. 'But – but I thought Mr. Mannering wanted to drive up to Yorkshire today,' she exclaimed.

'So he does,' replied Graham, frowning. 'There's plenty of time. Mr. Mannering doesn't need the

30

whole day to drive up to Hollingford.' He began to walk towards the kitchen. 'I'll just put these away,' he nodded at the vacuum cleaner and dusters, 'and then I'll see about getting you some breakfast.'

'Oh, no!' Domine put out a hand protestingly. 'I – I'm not hungry, thank you.'

Graham looked at her slim figure. Although she was above average height she was very slender and privately he thought she needed plenty of good food inside her. He bit his lip, and then said: 'You must have something. Lunch won't be ready for a couple of hours yet. How about a nice light omelette? Or some toast – or pancakes?'

Domine shook her head definitely. 'Oh, no, really. Per – perhaps a biscuit – and some coffee.'

Graham sighed. 'All right. Sit down, make yourself at home. I'll bring you a tray.'

'In here?' Domine glanced round expressively at the elegance of it all.

'Of course.' Graham gave a slight chuckle. 'Don't be so conscious of your surroundings!' His eyes were gentle. 'Mr. James often has a snack in here, when he's working on some manuscript or reading.'

Domine inclined her head, and after Graham had gone to see about the coffee, she walked over to a low table where a selection of the day's papers were strewn rather carelessly. She chose one at random, and sat down on a low chair by the wide window. The view was quite fantastic, although the rain was causing a faint mist to cover the city and she couldn't see far in the poor light. She concentrated on the paper, flicking through its pages without a great deal of interest. She wondered where James Mannering was this morning. Obviously, he was a very busy man, and she wondered how he could find the time to drive her up to Hollingford.

Reaching the theatre page of the paper, she scanned the plays currently being shown in the West End almost disinterestedly. Then his name caught her eye. A play of his called *The Inventory* was being shown at the Royal Duchess theatre. She folded the paper and read the description with avidity. Not that it told her much. It was simply a précis of what several newspapers had thought of the play, without any real criticism being involved.

She sighed, and turned the page almost reluctantly, wondering whether indeed the play was being a success. According to the article, it had good reviews, but that could mean everything or nothing, that much she knew. She tried to remember the name of the play she had seen with Great-Uncle Henry in Brighton, but her memory failed her. After all, that had been almost a year ago now, during the Christmas holidays. One thing was certain, it had not been *The Inventory*.

Graham returned with a tray on which was a jug of coffee, a jug of hot milk, some buttered scones and a selection of savoury biscuits. Thanking him, she took the tray to a low table and seating herself, said:

'Where is Mr. Mannering this morning?' in as casual a tone as possible, hoping Graham wouldn't sense her nervousness.

Graham stood regarding her solemnly. 'He's at the television centre,' he replied. 'They're putting out a play of his in a couple of weeks and he has some last-minute re-writing to do. The medium is different, you see. What is acceptable on stage is not necessarily acceptable on television, and vice-versa.' —

Domine listened with interest, and asked: 'Is this important for him? I mean – is it good to have a play on television?'

'Well, it rather depends,' replied Graham, warming to his subject. 'You see, a play going out nation-wide on a television channel reaches a hell of a lot of viewers and consequently having a play transmitted can kill it stone-dead, so to speak, theatre-wise.'

'I see.' Domine nodded slowly, taking a bite of a scone which was still warm and oozed with butter. 'And this play of Mr. Mannering's? Will this spoil it for the theatre?'

'No, not in this case. Actually, lately he's been doing quite a lot of writing for television for series work and so on. This is a play written several years ago which didn't have a great impact on the stage. The producer seems to think it will do better without the confines of stage production.'

Domine poured herself a second cup of coffee and nodded again. Obviously, Graham was intensely conscious of his employer's immense talent and took pride in his own knowledge of his work. She thought that she, too, might find his writing fascinating.

'Are – are you coming up to Yorkshire with us?' she asked now.

Graham shook his head vigorously. 'No, Miss Grainger. This is my domain. At Grey Witches they have quite enough staff as it is.'

Domine frowned. 'I thought perhaps – as you are sort of – well, what was it Mr. Mannering called you? A gentleman's gentleman!' She smiled. 'I mean – I thought perhaps you accompanied him everywhere.'

Graham looked rather amused. 'Mr. James is not the kind of man to take kindly to too much attention,' he replied. 'My previous employer, Lord Bestingcot, used me as his valet, but I'm afraid Mr. James won't submit to attentions of that kind.'

Domine finished her coffee and sighed with pleasure.

'That was delicious, Graham,' she said gratefully. 'I didn't realize I was so hungry.'

Graham looked pleased and lifted the tray. 'Well, it's almost twelve,' he said. 'Mr. James shouldn't be long. If you'll excuse me, I'll go and see about lunch.'

'Of course.' Domine nodded. 'I'll go and make my bed—'

'You'll do no such thing!' exclaimed Graham, horrified. 'That's my job. You take it easy. Look, there's the stereogram over there and plenty of records. Play that! Or find yourself a book to read. There's plenty on the shelves.'

Domine compressed her lips and allowed him his way. But she didn't like to admit that she didn't know how to work the stereophonic equipment, so she examined the books on the bookshelves, searching for something to take her interest.

There was a predominance of reference books among the hardback covers, but in the paperbacks there were thrillers and espionage stories, as well as several best-sellers which she glanced at rather tentatively, remembering what the other girls had said about novels that became best-sellers and their contents.

Then the telephone began to ring. It was a very modern affair in ivory, and as she had never answered a telephone before without being asked, she allowed it to go on ringing. However, after several moments, when it appeared that Graham either could not hear it or alternatively expected that she would answer it, she lifted the receiver and put it to her ear rather nervously.

'Hello,' she said softly. 'Who is that?'

'Is that Belgrave 04041?' asked a woman's imperious

voice.

Domine hastily examined the number on the centre of the dial. 'Y-yes,' she stammered, 'that's right.'

'Then to whom am I speaking?' questioned the woman sharply.

Domine hesitated. 'Er – my name is Domine Grainger. I'm Mr. Mannering's ward,' she replied. 'And if you want Mr. Mannering, I'm afraid he's not here.'

There was silence for a moment, and then the woman said: 'I see. Do you know when he'll be back?'

Domine glanced round and saw with relief that Graham had entered the room behind her. Putting her hand over the mouthpiece, she said: 'It's a woman. She wants Mr. Mannering.'

Graham frowned. 'Do you know who it is?'

Domine sighed and grimaced. 'Heavens, no.'

'Then ask her.'

Domine bit her lip and removed her hand. 'Who – who is calling, please?' she asked uncomfortably.

There was a stifled exclamation, and then the woman said: 'You can tell him it's Yvonne,' she said, rather angrily. 'Is he there? Won't he speak to me?'

'No!' Domine was horrified and replaced her hand over the mouthpiece again. 'She – she thinks Mr. Mannering is here and I'm preventing her from speaking to him,' she exclaimed.

Graham grinned. 'It must be Yvonne Park,' he said, knowledgeably, and Domine stared at him in surprise.

'Yes, she said her name was Yvonne,' she whispered.

'Then give it to me.' Graham held out his hand and Domine thankfully handed him the receiver, walking across the room to the window and trying not to take

35

any interest in the remainder of the conversation. But it was difficult when she had already heard part of the conversation and wanted to know the rest.

Graham handled the situation beautifully, she had to admit, but from his replies it was obvious that this woman did not believe that James Mannering was not in the apartment. However, Graham appeared at last to have convinced her, and affirmed that he would give Mr. Mannering her message as soon as he returned. As he replaced the receiver, he glanced across at Domine ruefully and said:

'That was unfortunate. However, Mr. James won't be here later in the day if she takes it into her head to come to find him.'

'Who – who is she?' asked Domine, flushing.

Graham heaved a sigh. 'Don't tell me you haven't heard of Park Textiles?'

'Park Textiles? You mean the manufacturers?'

'Yes. Yvonne is the daughter of Alexander Park, the chairman of the combine.'

'I see.' Domine sounded awed. 'Is – is she a friend of Mr. Mannering's?'

Graham gave a wry smile. 'You might say that. At any rate she'd like to be.'

'You mean Mr. Mannering isn't interested?'

Graham chuckled. 'His interest waned about six weeks ago,' he replied, walking towards the kitchen. Then he looked back at her almost compassionately. 'There are a lot of things you have yet to learn, Domine.'

Domine didn't object to his use of her Christian name. Instead, she sighed and dropped down into a low chair, cupping her chin on her hands. 'I expect Mr. Mannering has a lot of – well, women friends,' she murmured wistfully.

'Men and women aren't friends – they're antagonists!' remarked a lazy voice behind her, and she swung round to find that James Mannering had entered the apartment silently, and was standing leaning against the door jamb surveying her mockingly.

Graham chuckled, and withdrew, leaving Domine feeling at quite a disadvantage. She got awkwardly to her feet as he came into the room, and said hastily: 'There – there's been a call for you. From a woman called Yvonne Park.'

'Has there indeed?' Mannering flung himself into an easy chair and drew out his cigar case. 'Did you sleep well?'

'Did you hear what I said?' asked Domine, frowning.

'Yes, I heard,' he replied smoothly. 'Thank you for the message.'

'Sometimes,' she said, rather crossly, 'you make me feel very childish! You needn't act as though I wasn't aware of the facts of life. Graham told me that you and this woman used to be – well, friends!'

'Is that what he said?' Mannering got to his feet. 'How do you get along with Graham?' He poured himself a glass of whisky at the cocktail cabinet and went on: 'Don't imagine I'm a hardened drinker, will you?' he indicated the glass in his hand. 'It's just I've had rather an infuriating morning, and I'm not feeling exactly polite at the moment.'

Domine compressed her lips and turned away, sighing rather impatiently. He seemed determined to treat her as an infant.

Suddenly he said, rather surprisingly: 'I think we'll have to take you in hand, Domine.'

'What do you mean?' she asked defensively. 'If I'm not to discuss your affairs with Graham, then all right.

You needn't make a big thing about it.'

He smiled. 'What an aggressive little thing you are, aren't you? Or perhaps *little* is the wrong adjective.' He surveyed her rather mockingly. 'At any rate, I wasn't referring to my affairs – I was referring to your appearance.'

'My appearance?' she echoed, her cheeks colouring. 'What's wrong with my appearance?'

'There's nothing actually *wrong* with it,' he replied, consideringly, 'however, I don't find a navy blue pinafore dress and a white blouse particularly inspiring. Nowadays there are plenty of decent, attractive clothes to choose from, clothes with style and colour, that would do something for a girl like yourself.'

Domine put a hand on her plait awkwardly. 'Your father – Great-Uncle Henry, that is, didn't approve of ultra-modern clothes.'

'Nor do I!' he exclaimed impatiently. 'I'm not suggesting you should deck yourself out like some out-of-date hippie; nevertheless you do require something a little more decorative than school uniform to wear.'

'I have other clothes,' she retorted, somewhat shortly.

'Have you? Then by all means find something different and wear it.' He seemed to grow bored with the topic of conversation, for he poured himself a second drink and walking across the room, seated himself by the window with the pile of newspapers.

Domine compressed her lips, regarded the back of his head for several minutes, then turned and went into her bedroom, finding to her surprise that Graham must have entered through her bathroom, and her bed was made and the room was tidy again.

She opened her large suitcase and studied the contents without much enthusiasm. She hadn't the faintest idea what she could wear, and although, as she had said, she had other clothes, they were all rather sub-dued garments, in dark colours, and without a great deal of style. Eventually she chose a dark green velvet dress, with a close-fitting bodice and a pleated skirt, the sleeves of which were long and buttoned at the cuff. The colour did not complement the olive colour of her skin, and without make-up she looked pale and unin-teresting. She tugged the comb through her fringe and stared at herself gloomily. It was no good. She was not good-looking, and no amount of wishing would make her so.

When she emerged into the lounge, it was to find Graham there, talking to James Mannering, and as she closed the door, he said that lunch was ready. James Mannering stared at her with those piercing blue eyes, and then with an imperceptible shrug he allowed her to precede him into the dining-room.

During the meal he did not speak, and she could only assume that he was busy with his own thoughts. She supposed she ought to have discussed his morning's work at the television studios with him, but when he did not speak, she found the silence between them growing into an actual physical thing, and very soon she would not have dared to try to bridge it. Instead, she picked at the fried chicken and golden rice, and merely tasted the lemon soufflé that followed.

They had their coffee in the lounge, and as Domine was obviously expected to preside over the tray, she did so with nervous intensity, spilling her own coffee into its saucer and dropping the sugar tongs with an ignominious clatter. It was about one-thirty by this time, and she was beginning to think he had changed his mind about taking her to Grey Witches today. After all, he was a busy man, that much was obvious, and if he found the time to take her to Yorkshire then she need not expect that he would spend much time there with her. But what would she do? Would she be left to the care of his mother? The thought frightened her a little. After all, if she knew nothing of James Mannering, she knew even less about his mother and she did not imagine that Mrs. Mannering would approve of her son's new acquisition, an unwanted acquisition, some might say. She shrank within herself, leaning back in her chair feeling that awful sense of inadequacy assailing her again. All this, the apartment, her new surroundings, James Mannering himself, were a little too much for someone who had spent the last nine years in the cloistered atmosphere of a convent. Indeed she might have been better advised to take the faith and become a novice. At least it would not be a life alien to her.

James Mannering looked up from the papers he had been studying and regarded her rather impatiently, she thought. 'Now what thoughts are running through that agile brain of yours?' he questioned dryly.

Domine tried to appear nonchalant. 'Why – nothing,' she denied miserably.

He put the papers aside. 'Don't lie to me, Domine. Your face is as expressive as an open book.'

Domine lifted her shoulders. 'Well, I was just wondering whether you'd changed your mind about leaving for Yorkshire today,' she said jerkily.

He raised his dark eyebrows. 'No, I haven't changed my mind, why? Have you?'

Domine stared at him. 'You know very well my wishes don't count for anything,' she said shortly.

Mannering looked taken aback. 'What is that supposed to mean?'

Domine gathered strength from a rising sense of frustration. 'It doesn't occur to you, does it, that I might find the prospect of going to Yorkshire, of meeting your mother, rather terrifying!'

Mannering frowned. 'Why?'

Domine bent her head, twisting her hands together in her lap. 'Well, I'm not exactly used to a social round, Mr. Mannering. My days at the convent were very quiet ones, and the weeks I spent with Great-Uncle Henry followed a similar pattern.'

'And was it a pattern you enjoyed?' he asked, rather tautly.

Domine shrugged. 'Not – not exactly. Nevertheless, you can't expect to uproot someone from that kind of existence and expect them to immediately fit in to every pre-conceived idea you might have of them.'

'You don't want to go to Yorkshire?' he asked bleakly.

'It's not that,' she denied uncomfortably.

'Well, damn it, what is it?'

She sighed, her eyes shaded by the long lashes. 'I – well, I'm only just getting used to you, and now you're going to plunge me into an entirely different environment and expect me to get used to a whole lot of new people.'

He sighed exasperatedly. 'What would you have me do with you? You can't stay here!' His tone was flat and brooked no argument, but she dared to defy him.

'Why not?' she asked, looking up. 'At least – for a few days. Until I get used to everything. I – I could do some shopping. Great-Uncle Henry gave me a little money. I could use some of that and buy myself some clothes. I know you think I look a frump—'

'I didn't say that,' he interrupted her impatiently.

41

'You didn't have to,' she answered pathetically.. 'I could tell.'

Mannering rose to his feet and paced panther-like about the room. He ran a hand through his thick hair, and stared at her exasperatedly. Then he stopped and faced her. 'Look,' he said, 'what's frightening you about going to Yorkshire? My mother's no ogre! Besides, I'll be there.'

'Will you? Oh, will you really?' She got to her feet, clasping her hands together tightly. 'I – I thought you would just be taking me there and leaving me I – I know you're a busy man and I never dreamed you'd be taking time off to stay in Yorkshire, particularly as you have this television play coming off, and I know you said you'd had an awful morning when you came home before lunch, and then there's that Miss Park who's trying to reach you, and all your other friends, and naturally I thought you wouldn't have time to bother with me. . . .' She bit her lip, realizing she was chattering on unnecessarily, and that very likely he would be growing bored with her enthusiasm.

Mannering studied her animated expression and shook his head 'So that was your objection,' he murmured. 'Well, well, I appear to be in demand.' He smiled rather sardonically as she flushed. 'All right, all right, so you want to go to Yorkshire now, yes?'

'Yes.' Domine nodded slowly, not sure how to take his sarcasm.

'Good. Then I suggest we begin to make a start towards that end. Are your cases still packed?'

She nodded again, and he walked to the kitchen door and summoned Graham and proceeded to give him minute instructions as to the manner of explanation he should give to people who would be likely to call. Obviously, from the explanations he was giving, he had told his immediate associates what was going on, and it was only a question of supplying information to uninformed business acquaintances. Yvonne Park's name wasn't even mentioned, and Domine puzzled over this. Then they carried their cases to the lift which transported them down to the basement which housed the cars belonging to the tenants who occupied the apartments. Graham left them here, wished them a good journey, and took the lift back upstairs.

The previous day Domine had been too over-wrought to take a great deal of interest in her guard-ian's car, but today she noted with interest that it was a sleek luxury sports car of a continental variety with a speedometer that climbed to alarming heights of speed. However, she climbed inside obediently, and smoothed the skirt of her gaberdine over her knees. She was in-tensely conscious now of the limitations of her clothes, and realized that the overcoat James Mannering was wearing was lined with real fur and not a nylon imi-tation.

They drove out of the garages up a ramp on to the main thoroughfare, and eventually headed north up the Edgware Road towards Hatfield. It was still rain-ing steadily, and the windscreen wipers swished con-tinuously, while the tyres hissed on the wet road. In the environs of Greater London, Mannering did not speak, concentrating on the road ahead, and controlling the powerful engine he had beneath the car's bonnet. They stopped for traffic lights and occasionally he swore as another car swung dangerously across his path, but eventually they reached the motorway and he relaxed a little and gave the car its head.

He glanced at Domine, and said, 'Not much of a day to see your new home, is it?' and she shook her head.

'Is it my new home?' she asked curiously. 'I mean –

43

have you made any plans for my future?'

He shrugged, the wheel of the car sliding through his tanned fingers as he overtook a slow-moving furniture wagon. 'Not exactly plans,' he replied slowly. 'To begin with, you look as though you could do with a holiday, a real holiday, I mean, not those stiff visits you made to Crompton's Hotel.'

'You knew about them?'

'Sure. While you may have been kept in the dark about us, we were certainly not kept in the dark about you. You were my father's redeeming duty. You were the force that was to alter the selfish pattern of his life hitherto.'

Domine frowned. 'Tell me about your mother,' she said.

'What about her?' His voice was less relaxed when he spoke of his mother, as though he expected some kind of repudiation of her actions.

'Why didn't she marry Great-Uncle Henry after his wife and her husband died?'

Mannering gave a harsh mirthless laugh. 'My mother wouldn't marry Henry Farriday!' he exclaimed contemptuously. 'Not after everything that had happened.'

'What do you mean?'

He sighed. 'Oh, you'll learn soon enough, so I might as well tell you. My mother was not married when – when she became pregnant. She was working at Grey Witches then as a kind of assistant-housekeeper. Henry's wife was still alive, as I've told you. She held the reins of household affairs, and my mother liked her. Unfortunately, she succumbed to Henry's charm. Oh, he had charm all right, when he chose to exert it, and eventually the inevitable happened. I was the result!' He glanced at her wryly. 'It's shocking to you, isn't it?

44

A kind of bitter pill to swallow, being made the ward of Great-Uncle Henry's—'

Domine put her hands over her ears. 'Don't say it!' she cried, half angrily. 'It's not your fault!'

He shrugged. 'Well, anyway, when she found she was pregnant, she went to old Henry for help. Who else could she turn to? Who else was responsible? And do you know what he did? He turned her out! Just like that! Alone and friendless!'

'Oh, no!' Domine pressed a hand to her throat.

'Oh, yes. If it hadn't been for my father — for Lewis Mannering, that is — she'd probably have killed herself. As it was, Lewis married her, knowing all the facts of the case. My mother is nothing if not honest. I suppose in that respect I may take after her. I've never had any time for subterfuge.' He drew out some cigarettes and dropped them in her lap. 'Do you want one?'

Domine nodded, and lit one, her hands trembling a little as she used the lighter he handed her. Then he continued:

'It wasn't until years later that my mother became Henry's housekeeper, and by this time his wife was dead, of course.'

'But why did she do that?' Domine was puzzled. 'I don't understand why she should have gone back to him after the way he treated her.'

'Don't you? Well, perhaps not. But you'll learn as you go through life that there is such a thing as vengeance, and that was the reason why my mother went back. Old Henry didn't suspect, of course, when he employed her. It wasn't until afterwards when he saw me that he realized why she had done it.'

Domine was still bewildered. 'But where was your father?'

James Mannering sighed. 'My father was a farmer.

He only had a smallholding, but it was quite prosperous in its way, and when my mother married him she left Hollingwood and went to live with him near Beverley. I doubt very much whether Henry Farriday realized she actually had the child, you see. But unfortunately my father contracted cancer of the throat, and he died when I was only fourteen. That was when we went back to Grey Witches.'

'Oh, I see!' Domine began to understand. 'And Great-Uncle Henry recognized you.'

'Oh yes. Unfortunately, although I resemble my mother in temperament, my physique is wholly Farriday. You can imagine the stir it caused in the village, our living there, at Grey Witches, and nothing old Henry could do about it.'

'Why? Couldn't he have dismissed your mother?'

'I'm afraid my mother threatened to take the story to court should Henry refuse to support us,' replied Mannering, frowning. 'I don't say I agreed with her actions, but I could understand her motives. Later, when we were accepted, and the talk died down, I left Hollingford and went to London. The rest you know.'

'I see. And did – did your father want to acknowledge you – afterwards?'

'Oh, yes. He asked my mother to marry him several times. She always refused.'

'So that was why he left you the house – the estate.'

'Yes. I suppose you could say he achieved in death what he failed to achieve in life.'

Domine nodded and sighed, a feeling of trepidation assailing her. It was a story without compassion, unless one could feel compassion for the young woman his mother had once been. She wondered what Mrs. Man-

46

nering was like now, whether her bitterness had soured her beyond reproach. It was a strange and disturbing situation to a girl used to the uncomplex existence of convent life. She could hardly believe the man James Mannering was speaking about was the same kindly old gentleman who had made himself responsible for her on the death of her parents. And now here she was, on her way to stay with a woman who had lived her life in vengeance, and who must desperately love the son she had done everything in her power to have acknowledged.

CHAPTER THREE

DESPITE the driving rain and terrible driving conditions it was only a little after six-thirty when they turned off the motorway at Boroughbridge, taking the narrow road to Malton. After the comparative brightness of the lights on the motorway the winding road that led towards the north Yorkshire moors was dark and rain-washed, reminding Domine vividly of the country roads around the convent. They passed through a series of villages, that were little more than collections of lights in the darkness, before turning on to an even narrower track that led steeply upwards in a series of hairpin bends. It was rather frightening with only the headlights to guide them, and they were subdued by the wetness of the road, and only the knowledge that her guardian had complete control of the vehicle prevented her from clinging rather tightly to her seat.

At last they seemed to reach the summit of the hill, and even in the subdued lighting, Domine could perceive that ahead of them lay a stretch of barren, open country, without any sign of habitation of any kind. She guessed that they were on the moors now, and she wished it was daylight so that she could see where they were going. She had heard that the moors were beautiful, but right now, in the darkness and the pouring rain, they looked bleak and desolate, and wholly alien to her.

If James Mannering sensed her apprehension, he said nothing to reassure her, and not until they descended into a valley and the lights of habitation could be seen did he speak.

'That is Hollingford, up ahead,' he remarked, dispassionately. 'The house is about a mile beyond the village: It's quite a large estate, and my father owned most of the houses in the village, too.'

Domine nodded, trying desperately to think of something to say. For most of the journey a silence had prevailed between them, and she had been glad of it, busy with her thoughts after his startling revelations. She had no idea what thoughts had occupied his mind, but as he was a writer she imagined he would not find it difficult to entertain himself mentally.

Now he looked at her pale face, and said: 'Are you hungry? My mother will have dinner ready when we arrive.'

'Not particularly,' she confessed nervously. Then: 'Oh, you must know how nervous I am!'

He half-smiled. 'Don't be. No one's going to eat you, you know!' His fingers tightened on the wheel. 'At least, not while I'm around,' he amended mockingly, and she wondered what he meant by that remark.

They drove through the village, which was composed of a narrow street with some shops and houses, and a church with a school attached on the outskirts. Leaving the village behind they turned along a road lined with trees that dripped rain water heavily on to the roof of the car, and eventually reached double gates that stood wide with a small lodgekeeper's house at the side. But no one came out to ascertain their identity, and from the dereliction Domine assumed that the house was no longer in use. Instead, they continued up the drive towards the main building, and as it came into view, illuminated by the car's headlights, she felt a nervous sense of anticlimax. There was nothing beautiful about Grey Witches. Its stone façade was overgrown with creeper, and its windows were square-cut and unadorned. It was a double-fronted house reaching up some three floors and she thought it in no way resembled the gracious country home she had imagined.

James Mannering brought the car to a halt at the foot of a flight of steps leading up to the entrance and switching on the interior light he surveyed her face for its reaction. Seeing the disappointment mirrored there, he said:

'What did you expect? A National Trust property?'

Domine compressed her lips and shook her head. 'Of course not, Mr. Mannering. It – it's just different – from what I expected, that's all.'

He searched her face with those piercing blue eyes, and then without replying he turned out the light and slid out of the car. It was still raining, but not so heavily now, and when Domine slid out without waiting for his assistance she didn't bother to put up her hood to protect her head.

The house looked bleak and uninviting, and she shivered when no lights appeared and no one came to greet them, but James Mannering seemed unperturbed, and collected her cases from the boot, and mounted the steps to the front door.

Standing down his burden, he searched his pockets and brought out a handful of keys, one of which he inserted in the lock, and then pushing open the door he allowed her to precede him into the hall of the building. He leant across and switched on the lights, and immediately a huge chandelier overhead dispelled the gloom of the place. Instead, Domine saw that the hall was carpeted in red broadloom that spread up the staircase to one side of the entrance. Panelled walls were highly polished, and certainly there was no air of neglect here. The balustrade of the staircase curved to the upper regions of the house, and it was from this direction that there came the first sign that the place was habited. A girl came down the staircase swiftly to greet them, a girl older than Domine, probably in her middle twenties, Domine thought. She was fair and rather buxom, with fresh country cheeks, and a healthy outdoor appearance. Although it was early evening, she was still wearing jodhpurs, and Domine thought the masculine attire suited her athletic figure.

'James!' she exclaimed enthusiastically, rushing down the last few stairs to reach him, and grasping his lapels she kissed him soundly on his cheek. Domine had the feeling that the warmth of the girl's welcome was somehow for her benefit, but she had no way of knowing whether her suspicions were correct. At any rate, the girl drew back and looking at Domine said: 'Is this the girl?' for all the world as though Domine was incapable of answering for herself.

'Yes, Melanie,' murmured James, turning away from her interested eyes. 'This is Domine Grainger. Domine, this is Melanie Grant, my cousin.'

Domine shook hands politely, but she didn't much care for the speculative expression in Melanie's eyes, or the way she seemed to dismiss her as being beneath contempt. After the handshake, Melanie returned her attention to her cousin, helping him off with his coat and hanging it in the hall closet. Domine removed her gaberdine and with an amused glint in his eyes, James Mannering put it in the closet too. Then Melanie said:

'Come along, James, your mother has been waiting dinner for you for simply ages. She's in the conservatory now, watering the plants, and she can't have heard the car or she'd have been here to greet you.'

Domine followed James Mannering and his cousin through double doors into what appeared to be a large lounge. It was depressingly decorated in subdued colours, but a warm fire flickered cheerfully in the grate. Beyond this room was the dining-room, and through the open door Domine could see a maid putting the final adjustments to the table.

James allowed Melanie to take him through this lounge and the dining-room to where a glass-roofed conservatory could be seen. Domine saw the greenery of the plants, considered following them, and then changed her mind and waited instead in the lounge feeling rather like the skeleton at the feast.

Never in her wildest dreams had she thought of Grey Witches as being anything other than a charming house set in charming surroundings, but now, discovering this Victorian monstrosity set in country that was bare and saturated with rain and bore no resemblance to the green stretches of moorland she had envisaged, she felt unutterably depressed and miserable. She was wholeheartedly grateful that all this could only last for six months and wondered if Great-Uncle Henry had considered her feelings at all.

Voices could be heard coming in her direction and a moment later James Mannering re-entered the room with two women. One of them was, of course, Melanie Grant, but the other woman was older with dark hair that had reddish tints in its depths and was tall, slim and still rather attractive. Dressed in a chic dress of cream Crimplene with a slim-fitting skirt, she was the epitome of style and elegance, pearls encircling her veined throat, while there were rings on her long fingers. She was such an amazing anachronism in a house like Grey Witches that Domine couldn't prevent the gasp of pure amazement that escaped her. Happily no one seemed to notice, and Mrs. Mannering came forward to greet her, smiling in a seemingly friendly manner.

'So you're Domine, are you?' she murmured unnecessarily, studying her intently. 'Yes – you're as I expected you to be.'

Domine flushed, somehow aware that that was no compliment. 'Well, you're not at all as I expected,' she exclaimed candidly, but James Mannering's mother merely smiled in rather a complacent way, and said:

'Oh, did you hear that, James? The child's charming.' She looked again at Domine. 'I trust you did mean those words as a compliment,' she murmured rather chidingly.

Domine's coloured deepened. 'Of – of course, Mrs. Mannering. Somehow – I – well, I thought you'd look much – much older!'

'Did you now? And who gave you that idea? James?'

'Oh, no! Mr. Mannering didn't discuss your appearance at all,' Domine disclaimed hastily, and then realized what she had said.

'But he discussed me in other ways, I gather,' murmured Mrs. Mannering, glancing speculatively at her son. 'I wonder what he said. Are you going to tell me, Domine?'

'Leave her alone, Mother,' exclaimed James Mannering, as though bored by the trend of the conversation. 'You haven't asked her what kind of a journey she's had, or whether she's hungry or not. I expect she is. I didn't stop for afternoon tea on the way.'

'Typically you, darling,' replied Geraldine Mannering smoothly. 'But all right, I'll stop teasing you, Domine. You look rather tired, and I mustn't be naughty, must I? Now come along, dinner's just waiting to be served, so don't let's delay any longer. We can have a nice long chat after the meal.'

The meal was good. There was soup, hot, and thick with vegetables, the way Domine liked it, roast beef and Yorkshire pudding, and a raspberry pie and cream to follow. To her surprise, Domine found she was hungry, and she ate heartily, ignoring the rather cut-and-thrust conversation James Mannering held with his mother. It was apparent that their relationship had always been rather a stormy one, and Domine wondered whether that was because James was like his father or perhaps because he was more like his mother than either of them realized.

Inevitably, when dinner was over, and they retired to the lounge to have coffee, the conversation was directed towards Domine, and she was uncomfortably aware that she was the cynosure of three pairs of eyes. During the meal she had wondered what position Melanie Grant held in this household, and she had also pondered the ease with which Mrs. Mannering seemed to have adopted her role as mistress of the house. Considering her employer had only been dead for three weeks she seemed to have taken over quite completely. The maid who had served their meal, and who had later supplied them with coffee, had treated her mistress with deference, and that surprised Domine, who had imagined a quite different reaction.

Now Mrs. Mannering's eyes were upon her, and there was curiosity in their depths. Domine thought she must present a rather depressing picture to someone who obviously adhered very closely to the current trends of fashion. 'Tell me,' said Geraldine Mannering thoughtfully, 'did Henry ever speak of Grey Witches?'

54

Domine nodded. 'Sometimes, but I'm afraid he didn't mention any personalities.'

Mrs. Mannering frowned. 'And weren't you curious? I mean – surely in the – how many years was it? Nine? Ten?' She nodded. 'In all that time he was responsible for you he never brought you here. Didn't you wonder why?'

James Mannering intervened. 'Obviously she was curious!' he remarked dryly. 'But as you get to know the child you'll realize she's not the kind of kid to ask too many questions!'

Domine resented the disparaging way he dismissed her as a child, but before she could say anything, Mrs. Mannering said: 'Thank you, James, but I don't believe you are required to answer for Domine. She has a tongue in her head. She can answer for herself.'

James Mannering rose to his feet and going over to a side table where an array of drinks was laid out he helped himself to a whisky, and turning said: 'You're asking all the wrong questions!'

Mrs. Mannering looked up. 'Oh, yes?'

'Yes. Can't you see the kid's tired? Leave this catechism until the morning if you must discuss Henry at all. I've told you, she knows absolutely nothing about his affairs. She was his ward, he paid her school fees and at holiday time he took her away to Bognor, but apart from that – nothing!'

Mrs. Mannering lay back in her chair. 'Did he buy you those clothes?' she asked critically.

Domine flushed. 'Yes.'

'We must do something about your wardrobe while you're here, then,' said Mrs. Mannering, studying her appraisingly. 'After all, you're only young once, so they say.' She sat up straight again. 'Has James told you his plans for you?'

55

'Not now, Mother,' exclaimed James Mannering sharply, and a strange look passed between them before she shrugged gracefully, and said: 'Very well. I suppose it is a little late to start discussing your future tonight.' She turned to her niece. 'Melanie, my dear, do you have a pair of pants the child could wear in the morning? Some jeans or something. I don't suppose you have any trousers, do you?' This last to Domine.

Domine shook her head, and Melanie lifted her shoulders indifferently. 'I suppose I can find her something,' she agreed reluctantly. 'Why?'

Mrs. Mannering smiled slowly. 'Well, obviously, James will want to visit the horses while he's here, and as riding is the best way to see the estate, I imagine he will want to take his – *ward* – out with him in the morning.'

Domine's cheeks burned, and James looked slightly sardonic. 'Now what are you trying to achieve, Mother?' he asked exasperatedly, looking at Melanie, who Domine noticed didn't seem to care for the course of the conversation herself now.

'Why, nothing, darling,' Mrs. Mannering disclaimed charmingly. 'But you can hardly neglect your duties, can you?'

Domine opened her mouth to say something and then closed it again. She sensed that any protest on her part would be overridden by Mrs. Mannering, who seemed to be engrossed in some particular game of her own. Maybe she had a motive for offering invitations on behalf of her son, but right now Domine couldn't see what they were, unless, as Melanie looked so distressed, it was something to do with her. She couldn't conceivably imagine that by throwing her son and his ward together she would make Melanie jealous, did she? But no, that was ridiculous; she, Domine, was dismissed as being merely a child and therefore the only alternative, if Melanie was to join their ride, which seemed likely, was that Mrs. Mannering wanted to separate her niece and her son. It was all most disturbing, and Domine felt too tired to try and understand her jumbled impressions tonight.

Later, she said good night to her hostess and her son, and the scowling Melanie, and followed the maid upstairs. The house, for all its ugly outward appearance, was comfortably furnished, and if the appointments were dowdy and without much imagination, then at least they were not spartan, and the whole place was centrally heated. Her bedroom, which was on the first floor, was huge, with a high ceiling and an enormous four-poster bed which did not look out of place beside a mahogany tallboy and a dressing table with so many mirrors that Domine could see herself from every conceivable angle. The adjoining bathroom was old-fashioned, too, but the plumbing was adequate, and if the steaming water that poured from the polished brass taps was tinged with rust then at least it was hot.

She undressed, washed and cleaned her teeth, then climbed into the capacious bed. She turned out the light with the lazy-cord that hung over the bed and the room was plunged into pitch darkness. It was a trifle unnerving, being alone in such darkness, for at the convent she had shared a room with Susan and two other girls and although it had been dark there had at least been other human forms within a hand's reach. The rain beat incessantly against the windows and she heaved a sigh, wondering with a sense of despair whether it would ever stop raining, and then, because she had lain awake so long the previous night, she found her eyelids drooping, and presently she slept.

She was awakened by a bedside lamp being switched

on, and she struggled up on her pillows confusedly to find the maid who had shown her her room the night before presenting her with a tray of tea and biscuits. She was a very young maid, and she smiled mischievously at Domine, and said: 'Sorry if I startled you, miss, but Mrs. Mannering said to wake you at seven because you're going riding with Mr. James, is that right?'

Domine succeeded in maintaining a sitting position and stared at her watch. Rubbing her eyes, she smiled, and said: 'I can hardly believe it's that time. I seem to have just closed my eyes.'

The maid nodded understandingly. 'It's because it's still dark, miss, but it's beginning to brighten up already, and the rain has stopped.'

'Has it? Has it really?' Domine heaved a sigh. 'Thank goodness!' Then she noticed some clothes strewn on the bottom of her bed. 'What are those clothes?'

The maid smiled. 'It's some trousers, miss. Miss Melanie sent them. Mrs. Mannering asked her to give you something to wear to go riding.'

'Oh, yes.' Domine gulped her tea and thrusting the tray aside she jumped out of bed in her pyjamas and lifted the pants that were lying there. She held them against herself and grimaced at the maid, who was frankly giggling.

'Miss Melanie's more – more solidly built than you are, miss,' she exclaimed, biting her lips to quell her giggles. 'But if you pull the belt tight . . .'

Domine shook her head. 'Honestly, I think I'd rather just wear a skirt, except that that wouldn't look very ladylike, would it?'

'No, miss.' The maid lifted the tray and turned to go, but Domine stopped her.

'What's your name?' she asked, noticing for the first time how short the maid wore her clothes.

The maid halted. 'It's Lily, miss,' she said frankly.

'And how old are you, Lily?'

'Eighteen, miss.'

'Eighteen,' repeated Domine slowly. Lily was about her own height and build, and with a nervous linking of her fingers, she said: 'You – you don't happen to have an old pair of trousers I could wear, do you, Lily?'

'Me?' exclaimed Lily, then she smiled. 'Well, yes, I suppose I do. But I'm not sure whether Mrs. Mannering would approve of your borrowing trousers from me.'

'Oh, nonsense,' cried Domine, shaking her head. 'Heavens, you're the first young person I've met since I left the convent.'

'Mr. James and Miss Melanie aren't exactly old, miss,' murmured Lily doubtfully.

'I know, but – well, they're different, somehow,' replied Domine. 'Oh, please, Lily, hurry and get me something. I can't possibly go out in these!' She held the offending trousers against her again, and Lily nodded, dissolving into more laughter as she went.

Later, when Domine descended the stairs she realized how well trousers suited her tall slim figure. The pants Lily had lent her were made of whipcord, and were a kind of dust-colour, while the white shirt blouse she had worn for school looked far more suitable than the sweater Melanie had lent her. She carried a thick cardigan of her own, and thought she could wear that if she felt cold. Although it was October there had been no frost as yet, and she was looking forward to seeing something of her surroundings. She had learned to ride when she was a child, before the death of her parents, and although that was many years ago she didn't think she would have forgotten all she had learned. Besides she liked animals, and they invariably liked her.

In the hall she hesitated, not sure where to find her guardian, but as she hovered there looking rather young and attractive in the unusual garb, her plait falling over one shoulder, James Mannering himself emerged from the direction of the kitchen looking younger than she had previously seen him in riding breeches and a navy sweater.

He halted when he saw her, and a calculating look came into his eyes. 'Well, well,' he said, 'who'd have thought Melanie's gear would have become you so well!'

Domine compressed her lips. 'These are not your cousin's pants,' she admitted uncomfortably. 'They belong to Lily.'

'Lily Manvers?'

'If she's the maid, then yes,' replied Domine, flushing. 'Miss – Miss Grant's were too – too large for me!'

A smile broke his harsh features, and he ran a lazy hand over his dark hair. 'I rather thought they might be,' he murmured mockingly, 'however, I imagine that was part of my mother's plan, too.'

'What do you mean?' Domine looked bewildered, and he shook his head.

'You're to provide a distraction to the charms of my cousin,' he murmured sardonically, and she didn't know whether or not he was serious. 'Unfortunately, you're not supposed to provide an attraction as well,' he continued.

Domine couldn't understand a word of this, and she turned away in exasperation as Melanie Grant came down the stairs as she had done the previous evening, still wearing the same jodhpurs, but a different coloured sweater. She carried a small whip in her hand which she flicked against the knee-length boots she wore, and Domine realized she was only wearing thin-soled shoes. Still, she thought, she had no boots anyway, so there was no point in distressing herself on that account.

Melanie viewed Domine rather insultingly, then said: 'Good heavens, that isn't the outfit I sent you! Where did you get those cheap pants?'

James intervened smoothly. 'Lily lent her them,' he said. 'Yours – didn't fit!'

Melanie studied his expression, decided not to take offence and said: 'Oh, very well, shall we go?'

Outside, Domine had her first glimpse of Grey Witches in daylight and without the disguising sheet of rain. The sky was tinged the palest of pinks, and the clouds which had hung so heavily yesterday had dispersed to leave only a fleecy edging in the sky. The air was fresh and invigorating, with that wonderful smell of damp grass and vegetation, that seemed to add a subtle scent of its own. Smoke curled in the air from the chimneys of the houses down in the village which Domine realized now was some feet below them in the valley, while all around, outside the environs of the garden, stretched the violet-hued reaches of the moor. The colours dimmed from pastel green to deepest ebony and Domine felt her spirits rise excitedly. If the house had disappointed her, then certainly the moor did not, and she could not ever remember seeing so vast an area without any sign of habitation.

She found James Mannering by her side, and glanced at him nervously. 'Well?' he said. 'This is more like it, isn't it?'

'I – I think it's beautiful,' she confessed enthusiastically. 'The vastness – the desolation. It has a peace somehow.'

Melanie Grant turned to survey her impatiently. 'You've never had to live here when the snow piles high against the walls and we're cut off sometimes for weeks on end,' she said dampeningly.

'And nor have you,' remarked James Mannering, looking at her rather mockingly. 'And doesn't it rather depend with whom one is isolated? For instance, I can think of nothing more romantic than being marooned out here, on the moors, with nothing to do but eat and sleep and. . . .' He allowed the sentence to finish itself in the minds of his listeners, and Domine was aware of an unusual tingle running up her spine. His voice had been deep and husky, and when his eyes turned to hers she had the feeling he was deliberately using his undoubted expertise to arouse some kind of reaction, most probably in an attempt to tease his cousin. But instead, it was Domine who felt disturbed, and she was glad when Melanie flicked her whip and suggested they went round to the stables.

There were four horses in the stables; a bay gelding that the stableboy had saddled in readiness for Melanie, a grey, placid mare that was obviously a suitable mount for Domine, and two sleek hunters which looked the kind of mounts one would use to ride to hounds. James Mannering took one of these and suggested that Domine take the mare.

'She's a quiet animal,' he said, stroking the mare's muzzle. 'My father used to ride her sometimes. She was his favourite.'

'I thought that was your mother!' remarked Melanie tauntingly, mounted on the gelding which moved about restlessly in the stable yard.

Mannering looked up at her contemptuously. 'What

was that supposed to mean?' he asked harshly.

Melanie shrugged, flushing. 'Oh, nothing,' she said sulkily. 'Are you ready? If so, let's go!'

Domine was again conscious of the undercurrents here, and she was glad to mount the mare and taking the reins she dug in her heels and sent the animal trotting out of the yard. To her relief, the previous experience she had had kept her in good stead, and she kept up with the others easily as they left the drive of the house and gave the horses their heads across the moor.

It was exhilarating galloping along in the chill, morning air, the steam of their breath mingling with that of the horses. Domine had never felt such a sense of freedom and she decided to leave the others to their conversation and galloped on ahead, ignoring James Mannering when he called to her.

Over a rise, an exciting view awaited her. Away ahead, shimmering in the distance, was the sea, only a paler shade of blue than the sky in the morning light. A watery sun was rising and it made her raise her hand to shade her eyes from the glare. She found she was sweating a little herself from the exertion of controlling the mare, and she shed her cardigan, fastening it to the pommel and dismounting slowly.

An outcrop of rock provided an unexpected resting place, and she sat there feeling at peace with the world. The mare cropped the clumps of grass nearby, and there was a stillness that she had never before felt, not even in the chapel at the convent when she had requested to attend a service as a spectator.

She sighed and stretched, raising her arms high above her head in a completely natural gesture when she realized she was no longer alone. James Mannering had walked his horse over the rise and was standing on its brink watching her, with eyes that contained a most enigmatic expression. He did not look particularly pleased, and she wondered whether she had inadvertently trespassed on to someone else's property.

Colouring under his gaze, she rose confusedly to her feet and realizing that a button of her blouse had come loose as she was stretching she fastened it hastily, wondering whether he could hear the sudden pounding of her heart.

'I – I'm sorry,' she said, feeling that she must break the ominous silence that had fallen. 'Have you been waiting for me? Wh-where is Miss Grant?'

'Miss Grant has returned to the house,' he replied, at last, when she was beginning to think he wasn't going to answer her. 'What do you think you're doing, wandering off like this?' His tone was harsh.

Domine was amazed at the anger he was so obviously suppressing, and she couldn't begin to understand why her innocent expedition should have been misconstrued.

'I – I thought you and Miss Grant might prefer to be alone,' she faltered uncomfortably. 'I – I didn't imagine I was doing anything wrong.'

Mannering's brows drew together in a frown darkening a countenance that was already darkened by the sideburns that grew down his cheeks. Domine twisted her hands together, realizing that his attitude was doing something that she had hitherto not anticipated, that of making her aware of him not as her guardian, as a man old enough to be her father, but simply as a human being, a human male moreover, with human needs and desires. She shivered suddenly. Until this moment she had not appreciated the width of his shoulders, the muscular strength of his chest and litheness of his legs, but now she was conscious of the physical attraction of such a man, and it was not a comforting realization.

With jerky movements, she turned her back on him, and gathered the mare's reins preparatory to mounting.

James Mannering ran his fingers caressingly down his horse's neck, and said: 'In future you will ride with us, is that understood?'

Domine stared at him, for once shaken out of timidity. 'Why?' she asked sharply. 'Am I to be allowed no freedom?'

'Not on the moors, no. There are plenty of places where a man can hide here, hidden caves and gullies, where the canals used to flow under the moors, and still do in darkness. It could be dangerous!' His eyes flickered impatiently. 'Surely you have the sense to realize what could happen to you!'

Domine mounted the mare. 'I think you're deliberately exaggerating, Mr Mannering,' she said irritably. 'I don't know why, but something has angered you. Just don't make me the whipping boy for that kind of frustration!'

And with that comment she dug in her heels and sent the mare cantering away, leaving him still standing by his hunter. She was trembling when she reached the stables, and she was in no mood to cross swords with Melanie Grant, but obviously the other girl had been waiting for her.

'So James didn't find you,' she said, with some satisfaction. 'Riding off like that! What did you hope to achieve? A *tête-à-tête* with your guardian, perhaps?'

Domine brushed past her. 'Oh, don't be ridiculous!' she exclaimed impatiently.

Melanie caught her arm, preventing her escape. 'Yes,' she said, surveying Domine insultingly, 'I suppose it is ridiculous really. Little mouse, what on earth was old Henry doing putting you on James's conscience? A sort of – love me, love my dog situation, isn't it? Or in your case – inherit my house, inherit my great-niece!' She laughed mockingly. and Domine stood, staring at her uncomprehendingly.

'What do you mean?' she asked unsteadily.

Melanie gave a smirk of satisfaction. 'Don't you know? Of course, James would keep a thing like that to himself!' She turned and slapped the rump of her horse so that it moved a trifle protestingly.

Domine caught her arm. 'Tell me!' she said; then appealingly *Please!*'

Melanie's expression softened a little. Then she sniffed. 'Well, I suppose I might as well. Aunt Geraldine is bound to let it slip sooner or later. Your name wasn't mentioned in Henry Farriday's will. But the solicitors knew of your existence, and as there were only six months to go to your reaching the age of independence, James agreed to become your guardian in place of his father!'

CHAPTER FOUR

For a moment after Melanie had finished speaking Domine just stared at her, her eyes wide and disbelieving and yet already mirroring the pain she was feeling. Melanie seemed instantly to regret that she had spoken so rashly, and in an attempt to distract Domine's attention from her revelations, she shaded her eyes and said: 'Why, here's James coming now. He'll be relieved to see you've got back safely.'

Domine stared at her a moment longer, glanced once in the direction Melanie had indicated, and then with a muffled sob she ran blindly across the stable yard, and into the house, panting as she sped up the stairs to the comparative sanctuary of her room. Once there, she sank down shakily on to her bed and buried her face in her hands. Oh, God, she thought despairingly, so that was why he had found her such an encumbrance. He had not expected or wanted a ward, and his treatment of her, a mixture of impatience and gentleness, had been merely a front to hide his real feelings. Only today, on the moors, he had shown she was merely a nuisance to him, someone who deserved his contempt for being so utterly reliant upon him.

She pressed the palms of her hands against her cheeks, feeling unutterably miserable. So much had happened since she left the convent two days ago, so many complex problems had arisen, so many undercurrents had become apparent to her, and she was not equipped to deal with them. Even now, she had barely touched the surface of the man who was her guardian, whether of his own volition or otherwise. These three people into whose lives she had unwillingly been thrust all had involvements of their own and she was the least knowledgeable of them all.

She got unsteadily to her feet and as she did so caught a glimpse of herself in the many mirrors of the dressing table. She looked different somehow, and she realized it was the trousers Lily had lent her which gave shape to her slim hips and slender legs. The blouse was taut across her rounded young breasts and she realized with almost a sense of shock that she looked less of a child and more of a woman. Was that how James Mannering had seen her? Was that just another thing to annoy him, the realization that she could not be dismissed to the schoolroom like a child could have been?

She turned away from the mirror. Whatever her feelings she could not stay in her bedroom indefinitely, and presently no doubt someone would come to make the bed and tidy the room. After breakfast she would have to get around to unpacking her clothes, but right now she must make herself look less flushed and wind-blown.

She unfastened her hair from its confining braid and taking a brush she began to smooth it over her shoulders. It was amazing how much frustration could be dispelled by that simple action, and she tried not to think of the implications of Melanie's revelations. How could she stay here now, knowing he had merely taken pity on her? Somehow she must get away, make a life for herself, get a job! Oh, how thoughtless Henry Farriday had been, disregarding his guardianship of herself completely. Even if he had only left enough money to enable her to finish her schooling, she could have managed.

68

She was in the process of considering what her first actions should be when there was a knock at her door. Thinking it was Lily, she called 'Come in' and continued to brush her hair. Thick and silky, it fell straight and smooth, framing her face and drawing attention to the darkness of her eyes.

But when the door opened it was not Lily Manvers who entered the room but James Mannering, looking dark and angry, those naked blue eyes raking her mercilessly. He closed the door, and she rose from her seat at the dressing table feeling suddenly disturbed by his intervention into her thoughts. She was intensely conscious of her unbraided hair and tear-stained appearance, and she held back her hair from her face and faced him with apprehension.

Mannering ran a hand through his own hair, then said rather huskily: 'I want to know what Melanie told you in the stable yard that caused you to dash up here just now as though the devil himself was at your heels.'

Domine pressed a hand to her throat, shaking her head. 'I – I'd rather not talk about it just now,' she said, compressing her lips. 'I haven't had – had time to consider it.'

'Oh, for the Lord's sake!' he exclaimed. 'I know what she said!'

Domine coloured. 'Then why ask? You must know how I felt. She – she merely clarified your position, that's all. Now I need time to clarify mine.'

He put his hands on his hips. 'There's no clarification needed,' he snapped shortly. 'It doesn't make the slightest bit of difference.'

'Oh, but it does,' she contradicted him unsteadily. 'I – I can't stay here now. I don't want your charity. I'm quite capable of getting a job—'

'You think so?' His tone was sardonic and cold.

'I know so.' She turned away, biting her lip to stop it from trembling. It had been bad enough before, but this was worse.

There was silence for a moment, and Domine took a deep breath. Then he said in a quiet voice that nevertheless brooked no argument: 'Now, I'll tell you what you're going to do, shall I?' When she did not answer he continued: 'You are going to forget every word that Melanie said. She's not so bad when you get to know her, but like my mother, she's grown used to fighting for what she wants, and she's forgotten there are still people in the world who are not tarred with the same brush.'

Domine bent her head. 'You can't make me stay here,' she said tightly.

'Oh, but I can,' he muttered icily.

'I'm nothing to you. I'm not even your ward.' Domine swung round. 'I should have thought you would have been only too glad to discharge your responsibilities!'

He glared at her. 'What is that supposed to mean?'

Domine stiffened her shoulders. 'I don't want to stay here, anyway. I've met nothing but antagonism since I came. You're not going to pretend your mother would care if I left.'

He stepped towards her, his eyes brilliant with his frustration that she should cross him in this. Maybe he had thought she was like a pawn on a chessboard, thought Domine – silent and helpless, willing to be moved when it suited him. Now he had discovered she had a will of her own.

'Has our treatment of you been so terrible?' he asked harshly.

Domine's colour deepened. 'No, of course not. But I'm in the way here—'

'Who said so?'

Domine shook her head. 'Why didn't you just leave me in the orphanage?' she asked unhappily.

His eyes were glitteringly close to hers. 'Because I was foolish enough as to imagine you might be glad to leave an institution for a proper home life,' he bit out furiously.

'Here?'

'Where else?'

Domine lifted her shoulders. 'And if I still want to go?'

'Then I should have to think of some method of preventing you,' he replied. 'And believe me, I would find some way.'

'But why?'

'Because I have no intention of turning an innocent like you loose on the world. As I told you before, my father would have gauged my reactions. He never did anything without reason.'

Domine looked distressed. 'He took me out of the orphanage when I had no one,' she reminded him.

'So he did! And we've still not discovered why!'

'You're impossible!' she exclaimed. 'No one can be so unfeeling about their own father!'

He gave her a derisive stare. 'You think not.' He shrugged. 'In any event – you will stay. What have you to lose? In six months I'll be unable to prevent you leaving.'

Domine nodded. 'We'll see.'

'Damn you, don't fob me off with your temporizing!' he snapped, grasping her shoulders in hard, unyielding fingers. 'I've said you're to stay, and you will stay. Yes?'

Domine caught her breath in her throat. Although his fingers were bruising the flesh of her shoulders she did not try to struggle free. She had not been this close to him before and she could feel the heat of his body that was almost touching hers and see the darkness of the hairs that grew above the open collar of his shirt. His eyelashes veiled his expression and she thought how long they were, and how dark against the blueness of the pupils. A gold watch encircled one wrist while a ruby signet ring sparkled on the small finger of his right hand.

'You're hurting me,' she said chokingly, and immediately she was free, although she was aware he was staring at her with a strange look on his face.

'I'm sorry,' he muttered harshly. 'But you angered me.'

Domine shivered. 'I'm sorry, too,' she murmured.

'And you *will* stay.' It was a statement, not a question.

'Very well.' She felt strangely exhausted and had not the strength to fight him any more today.

'Good.'

Without another word, he turned and left the room, and after he had gone Domine felt limp. Never before had she realized the emotions that could be involved between a man and a woman, and there was a stirring sense of elation inside her that had nothing to do with anything she had ever before experienced.

With an impatient shrug she thrust these thoughts aside, but she was beginning to realize that life with James Mannering could never be dull. She wondered what thoughts had run through his mind as he had stood staring at her so strangely. Had it all been anger, or had he realized, too, that she was flesh and blood and feelings?

72

Later, after she had re-braided her hair, she went and washed before breakfast, removing the pants Lily had lent her and replacing them with the velvet dress she had been wearing the night before. In spite of the outdated clothes and uninspiring colours she could see a faint colour in her cheeks, and she did not look quite so drab as she had done the previous day. Certainly, plenty of fresh air would remove that pallor from her cheeks for good. And if James Mannering wanted her to stay at Grey Witches why should she refuse? Somehow, now, she felt more capable of facing Mrs. Mannering and Melanie, and after all, Henry Farriday had taken it upon himself in the first place to remove her from the orphanage and the care of the welfare societies. Had she remained in the orphanage this situation would never have arisen and therefore she could not be held entirely to blame for it, could she?

As she fastened the buttons of her dress she thought she might be able to buy a pair of trousers at the village shop. If she was to stay here, she would have to have a pair. They were the most suitable gear for going about the farm, and she had no intention of spending her days indoors.

It took quite a deal of courage to go down to breakfast, however, but when she got there she found her guardian was not present at the table. Only Melanie Grant and Mrs. Mannering were there, and as they were smoking cigarettes with cups of strong black coffee, they had obviously almost finished. They both looked at her a trifle cautiously as she entered the dining-room and for a moment she thought that the disturbed tenor of her mind must somehow reveal itself in her face.

Wishing her hostess good morning, she seated herself at the table, but when Lily came to ascertain her needs she asked only for toast and coffee. She waited, hands folded, wishing she could think of some bright topic of conversation, but happily Mrs. Mannering had no such difficulty.

'Did you sleep well?' she asked, and Domine nodded and said she had. Then Mrs. Mannering went on: 'You went riding with James and Melanie; did you enjoy that too?'

Domine bent her head. 'Very much,' she replied quietly, realizing that Melanie was regarding her with some small amount of anxiety, and she wondered whether the older girl was still wondering what the outcome of her spiteful revelations might be.

Mrs. Mannering bit her lip. 'It's strange that James should have forgone his breakfast this morning,' she ventured, glancing speculatively at each of her companions. 'He usually enjoys a good meal after an energetic ride over the moors.'

Melanie sighed. 'I expect he'll make up for it later,' she said broodingly. 'You know very well he takes half his meals in the kitchen while he's here. After all, he's more used to that part of *this* house, isn't he?'

Mrs. Mannering's bland expression hardened. 'Are you trying to say something, Melanie?' she asked softly.

Melanie coloured. 'If I am, I meant nothing by it,' she denied swiftly. 'You know it's true! James never wanted to eat in here! It brought back too many memories, he said!'

'James says a lot of things that should not be taken too seriously,' remarked Mrs. Mannering icily, 'as no doubt you'll already have gathered, Melanie.'

Melanie pushed her cup aside. 'Yes, he takes after you in that respect, dear aunt,' she returned offensively. 'Particularly when it comes to getting what he wants!'

Mrs. Mannering was obviously controlling her temper with difficulty. 'I think, Melanie, that we should not discuss such personal matters in front of our – guest.' She ran her tongue over her lips. 'After all, our petty bickering can be of no interest to Domine.' She smiled at Domine. 'What are your plans for this morning, my dear? Have you thought about what you'd like to do?'

Domine accepted the toast and coffee Lily brought in at that moment and intercepted a rather amused gleam in Lily's cheerful eyes. Obviously she was used to the uneasy relationship that existed between her mistress and her mistress's niece.

'I haven't made any actual plans,' Domine said now, buttering herself a slice of toast, the argument between Mrs. Mannering and Melanie successfully dispelling her own feeling of depression. 'But I should like to see the village, and I thought I might walk down there after breakfast.'

Mrs. Mannering considered this. 'Yes, I think that's quite a good idea. This afternoon, though, we must devise some kind of occupation for you. This is a lonely place, and there isn't a lot to do short of reading or watching television. There are the horses, of course, but one can't spend all one's days riding, can one?' She glanced rather meaningly at Melanie's usual attire of riding gear, and again Domine sensed the antagonism.

Melanie rose to her feet. 'There are always the stalls to be cleaned out,' she remarked dryly. 'Would you have me wear the kind of garments you favour for mucking out the pigs?'

Mrs. Mannering gave a distasteful gesture. 'Really, my dear Melanie, you're getting far too touchy! Did I say anything that gave you to understand I was chiding you?'

Melanie grimaced. 'You didn't have to, dear aunt. I know you of old.'

'Oh, for heaven's sake, Melanie!' Mrs. Mannering's delicately lacquered nails bit into the tablecloth. 'Go and do your mucking out – or whatever it is you're waiting to do. I shan't stop you!'

'I'll bet you won't.' Melanie strode to the door and then turned. 'Just remember, your petty jibes are like water off a duck's back!' She snorted mockingly. 'Half of the pleasure in James's presence is the knowledge that while he's here at least I'm not the only brunt of your machinations!'

'Oh, stop it, Melanie!' Geraldine Mannering was really angry now, and there were two bright flags of colour in her cheeks. 'You know perfectly well that Reuben and Brian can handle all the farm work there is to be done. Your predilection for burying yourself in manure and coming in here smelling like the piggery is no concern of mine!'

'And you know perfectly well that without my help the stables would never be touched!' Melanie stormed at her.

'Well, the horses are unnecessary now, anyway. James isn't here frequently enough to warrant their keep!'

'Oh, you – you—' Words failed Melanie, and she turned and banged out of the room.

After she had gone it took Geraldine Mannering several minutes to re-assume the smiling countenance she had previously displayed, and Domine whose appetite had been dispersed by the argument she had just uncomfortably been the witness to poured herself a second cup of coffee and wondered how she could fool-

76

ishly have imagined that Grey Witches would be a home to her.

Geraldine eventually regained her composure, and smoothing the tablecloth rather nervously, she said: 'You must excuse Melanie, my dear. She does get rather overwrought when I tackle her about her appearance.'

'Did you?' asked Domine, fingering her cup thoughtfully. 'Tackle her about her appearance, I mean.'

Mrs. Mannering frowned. 'What do you mean?' she asked, rather sharply.

'Well, I didn't think Melanie was involved – at least, not until she involved herself, that is.'

Mrs. Mannering hesitated a moment. 'Well, yes, I suppose you're right, but Melanie is aware of my displeasure regarding her mode of dress, and any kind of suggestion from me that those horses are in jeopardy brings forth a veritable tirade.'

'Does – does she help about the farm?'

'Yes. You see, although this is a large estate, run by an estate manager who you'll meet eventually, we have retained enough land to provide a kind of home farm. The estate stretches for many acres, you understand, and much of this is run by the tenants. Did James explain any of this to you?'

'He said his – his – father had owned most of the houses in the village,' stammered Domine, rather uncomfortably, and Mrs. Mannering gave a rather sardonic smile.

'You seem to have difficulty in accepting that James is your great-uncle's son,' she remarked mockingly.

'Why – no, that is – I—' Domine was at a loss for words. 'Won't you go on about the farm?' she suggested. 'I – I – am interested.'

77

Mrs. Mannering looked as though she would have liked to have said more, but instead she accepted Domine's suggestion and continued: 'Well, it's true to say that Henry was the biggest landowner hereabouts.' She found this knowledge very satisfying, that Domine could tell from her expression. 'But it's the land immediately surrounding the house that we are discussing, aren't we? You see, when Henry was alive both the house and the land were adequately tended by his staff. Unfortunately, on his death, some of the servants found it difficult to accept me as mistress here, and naturally they had to be dismissed.'

'Naturally,' echoed Domine inaudibly.

'Lily was different. She's been here only a couple of months and felt she owed no particular allegiance to Henry Farriday. The cook is new. She's a very capable woman from Leeds, and between us we manage to maintain the part of the house we are now using. Of course, you haven't seen over the place yet, but it's quite monstrously large, much too big really for anyone. But I like it.' She relaxed in her chair complacently.

'And Melanie?' ventured Domine quietly.

'Melanie? Ah, well, Melanie is the daughter of my late sister. When my sister died two years ago and Melanie was left alone in the world, I suggested to Henry that she might be allowed to come here and live with me. He agreed, and originally she intended to take a job in Helmsley or perhaps Whitby. There is transport to these places, you know,' this as a kind of aside from the main subject of her discourse, and Domine nodded, wondering whether there was some other reason for advising her of this fact. However, Mrs. Mannering went on: 'But when it became apparent that Melanie enjoyed working with the animals, Henry suggested that she might care to take on the job of exercising the horses. Of course, one thing led to another, and after some of the staff left when Henry died, I'm afraid Melanie had to help in other ways.'

'The pigs?' murmured Domine, a dry note in her voice, and Mrs. Mannering shrugged her slim shoulders.

'Someone has to do it,' she said indifferently. 'And staff are very hard to come by in an out-of-the-way place like Hollingford. Nowadays, the young folk make for the cities. Henry's staff were all middle-aged or elderly. They didn't know any other kind of life.'

Domine was beginning to understand. She could even feel a kind of sympathy for the absent Melanie. She wondered why she stayed here, treated with such contempt by her aunt, and then she realized what compelled Melanie to live under such conditions. It was James Mannering, of course. She ought to have thought of that at once, but somehow she doubted whether Geraldine Mannering would consider her a suitable applicant for the position as her son's wife. No, the more Domine thought about it, the more convinced she became that Mrs. Mannering would have her eyes set on higher planes. She was an ambitious woman, her position here proved that, and while she might argue with her son, and disagree with some of his actions, basically, in her eyes, he could do no wrong.

Domine finished her coffee and rose from the table. 'Well, Mrs. Mannering,' she began awkwardly, 'as there's so much to be done, perhaps I could help – while I'm here.'

Mrs. Mannering's eyes flickered. 'While you're here,' she echoed pensively, and Domine felt sure she was considering whether or not to enlighten her son's ward as to her actual position at Grey Witches. Then she said: 'Yes, I think that might be a good idea,

Domine, a very good idea indeed.'

Domine enjoyed walking down to the village later in the morning. It was quite a pretty village with its beautiful old church and weathered buildings. In the general stores she was able to purchase a pair of cheap jeans which she thought would do to wear about the farm, and also some writing materials and stamps to enable her to write to Susan. She thought the other girl might be interested to learn how she was progressing with her famous playwright. She smiled wryly. No exciting London life for her, just a rather nebulous position in a farming household, where everyone seemed to be at each other's throats.

When she returned to the house there was a Land-Rover parked at the front entrance, and she looked at it curiously as she mounted the steps and entered the hall. She had hoped to escape to her bedroom without being seen, but Mrs. Mannering was standing in the hall, talking to a young man, and when she saw Domine she indicated that she should join them.

'So there you are, Domine,' she said smilingly. 'I want you to meet the estate manager, Vincent Morley. Vincent, this is the late Mr. Farriday's great-niece.'

Vincent Morley was tall and stockily built with thick fair hair and a good-natured countenance. Now he glanced at his hostess, and said:

'Isn't this James's ward?'

Mrs. Mannering's smile vanished. 'Yes, of course,' she said disagreeably, 'but the relationship is still the same.'

Vincent Morley inclined his head and shook Domine's hand warmly. 'I'm very pleased to meet you,' he said in a friendly fashion. 'When did you arrive?'

'Yesterday evening,' replied Domine, returning his smile.

'And are you staying long?' he inquired.

Domine shrugged her shoulders. 'I'm not really sure, Mr. Morley. It depends – it depends on what plans my – my guardian has made.'

Vincent nodded. 'I see. Well, I hope to see you about the place if you do stay for any length of time, and if you want a conducted tour I'd be happy to offer my services.'

'Thank you,' Domine smiled, and the young man and Mrs. Mannering moved towards the front door, continuing the discussion they had been having before Domine's arrival. Domine waited until they were looking the other way, and then sped up the stairs to her room. She had no desire to have yet another conversation with Mrs. Mannering at the moment.

In her room, she found her suitcases had been unpacked for her and her clothes hung away in the capacious wardrobe. Looking at them, she felt a sense of dissatisfaction assail her. While it had not seemed important to wear anything attractive in the convent she felt that here she looked terrible in drab school garments. Even those clothes that Great-Uncle Henry had seen fit to provide her with were thick and out-of-date, and she wondered whether there was any chance of her obtaining some new clothes.

Glancing at her watch, she saw that she still had almost an hour before lunch and with sudden decision she extracted one of her dresses from the wardrobe. It was a mustard-coloured jersey with long sleeves and a loose appearance that was given shape by a tie-belt. Laying it on the bed, she studied it critically, remembering with clarity the smartness of Lily's uniform, cheap or otherwise.

At the bottom of her suitcase she found a pair of scissors, and with drastic decision she cut six inches off the hem of the dress. Then she found her sewing kit and sat on the bed, hemming a neat edge round the bottom of the skirt. This done, she held it against herself. It was certainly shorter than anything she had ever worn, but she didn't think it was too daring. Then she studied the style. There wasn't much she could do about it except to make a couple of tucks in the bodice to give it a little shaping. She discarded the belt altogether and with trembling fingers she stripped off the velvet dress and put the mustard dress on.

To her astonishment and satisfaction it looked not at all bad, and the colour was bright enough to complement the darkness of her complexion. She applied a coral lipstick to her lips and stood back to get the full effect. Of course her hair still looked childish, but she didn't consider herself old enough to wear it in a knot on top of her head. That would look quite ridiculous, and besides, she wasn't trying to look older, just less dowdy.

Lily's summons to lunch came soon afterwards, and with some trepidation Domine left her room. Happily both Mrs. Mannering and Melanie were already seated at the table on her arrival, and only James Mannering was still in the lounge, a glass of whisky in one hand, and a sheaf of papers in the other. He barely glanced at Domine as she entered, and she hastened across to the door of the dining-room, hoping to pass unnoticed. But just as she thought she had made it, his voice halted her.

'Good God!' he exclaimed, swallowing the remainder of his drink in a gulp. 'What in the devil's name have you been doing to yourself?'

Domine turned slowly. 'I don't know what you

mean,' she said reluctantly. 'I haven't done anything to myself.'

'All right, then, split hairs,' he grunted moodily. 'I mean that dress! Great-Uncle Henry would never have spent his money on anything like that!'

'James, for goodness' sake, what is going on?' called his mother's petulant voice from the dining-room. 'Is Domine down yet?'

'Yes, Mother,' James's tone was resigned as he looked at Domine with brooding blue eyes. 'What is this all about?' he asked, in a low tone. 'What has brought on this urge for a *mini*-rebellion?' He chewed his lip. 'I hope you didn't misconstrue what happened this morning—'

Domine, who had been maintaining her composure with difficulty, now turned scarlet. 'Don't flatter yourself, Mr. Mannering!' she snapped, and turning she flounced rather jerkily into the dining-room.

James followed her after a few moments, but now Melanie's alert gaze had appraised Domine's appearance and she raised her eyebrows in surprise.

'Well, well,' she said mockingly. 'The cuckoo is beginning to sprout wings. And so quickly, too!'

Mrs. Mannering compressed her lips. 'Really, what are you talking about, Melanie? Domine, are you all right? You look almost feverish!'

Melanie seemed to find the whole situation vastly amusing. 'Your son's – er – *protégé* has modernized her appearance, Aunt Geraldine,' she remarked sardonically. 'I wonder why?'

Domine clenched her fists. 'All I've done is shorten the skirt of this dress, Mrs. Mannering,' she protested hotly. 'Good heavens, does everyone have to make a federal case out of it?'

Mrs. Mannering glanced at her son doubtfully. 'No

one's making any kind of case out of it, my dear,' she said, rather tautly. 'But I would be interested to learn why you should have done such a thing.'

Domine's colour deepened. 'Everyone keeps telling me I'm only a teenager,' she exclaimed. 'Very well, then, Lily's a teenager, too, and her skirts are short!'

'I see.' Mrs. Mannering twisted her wedding ring round her finger. James Mannering seemed deep in thought. He had apparently helped himself to another drink and now sat swirling the liquid round in his glass with assumed concentration. Melanie was drinking her soup with obvious enjoyment, and Domine realized she was really appreciating the lighter aspects of the situation.

'You must understand that your position in this household is much different from that of Lily Manvers,' Mrs. Mannering said eventually.

Domine frowned. 'I know that.'

'Very well then, just because Lily chooses to dress in a rather – how shall I put it? – common manner, there is no reason why you should do the same.'

Melanie finished her soup and pushed her plate aside. 'What's wrong, Aunt Geraldine?' she taunted lightly. 'Afraid of the competition?'

Domine was beginning to realize that in this instance she had an ally in Melanie, and she wondered why. She didn't imagine that Melanie's opinion of her had changed during the course of a morning, but by siding with Domine Melanie was, in some way, getting back at her aunt for her earlier digs at herself.

James Mannering looked bored in the extreme, and interrupting them, he said quietly: 'I have some work to do this afternoon. Is the typewriter still in the study, Mother?'

'Yes, dear.' His mother frowned. 'Surely you're not

84

going to write here, James!'

He gave a sardonic shake of his head. 'There's not much chance of that with you two rowing all the time,' he remarked dryly. 'Just don't make Domine another excuse for your petty bickering!'

Domine glanced at him, finding his eyes upon her, but there was no warmth in them, and she realized with a sense of depression that he was merely speaking on her behalf out of politeness.

Suddenly Lily appeared, looking rather agitated. 'Excuse me, sir,' she said, addressing James Mannering, 'but a visitor has arrived for you.'

James looked up sharply. 'Who? Did you tell them I was here?'

'Of course she did, darling,' drawled a lazy voice, a voice which to Domine sounded vaguely familiar. 'And why not? You are here, aren't you?'

James got to his feet, and Domine swung round to see one of the most beautiful young women she had ever seen in her life standing in the doorway to the lounge. She was dressed in a midi-length coat of jade green with an edging of silver fur at the collar and hem. A silver fur hat adorned her blonde head, while she carried a silver muff. She wore knee-length boots of soft black leather, and carried herself with style and elegance. Certainly, she presented an incongruous picture among Great-Uncle Henry's Victoriana, thought Domine, wondering why the sight of her should arouse such a sense of antipathy inside her.

James went to meet her, but his voice was cold and there was no enthusiasm in his greeting. Then he turned. His mother was standing, too, now, and Domine observed a look of real pleasure on her face before James said:

'Domine, this is Yvonne Park. You remember? You

85

spoke to her on the telephone at the flat. Yvonne, this is my ward, Domine Grainger.'

His method of introduction was not lost on Mrs. Mannering, and her eyes hardened when she looked into her son's bored countenance. Then, she moved forward welcomingly, smiling warmly.

'My dear Yvonne,' she enthused. 'How lovely to have you call so unexpectedly. I didn't even know you were in Yorkshire. James never said anything. The last I heard you were in London.'

Yvonne's eyes flickered. Apart from a polite smile at Domine, which was supposed to encompass Melanie too, she ignored them completely, concentrating her whole attention on James Mannering and his mother.

Under cover of their conversation, Melanie glanced meaningly at Domine. 'Yvonne Park of Park Textiles,' she murmured, in an undertone. 'Can't you see Aunt Geraldine almost genuflecting?'

Domine frowned. 'I thought—' She halted. 'Mr. Mannering wouldn't speak to her when she rang the apartment in London,' she whispered.

Melanie shrugged. 'That doesn't surprise me. He's been trying to shake her off his back for months. But Aunt Geraldine is a stayer, I'll say that for her, and she's determined to make her son part of the Park millions!'

Domine looked puzzled. 'What do you mean?' she breathed.

Melanie sighed. 'My aunt is an ambitious woman, and right now she's involved in the biggest deal of her life. Yvonne is to be the future Mrs. James Mannering.'

Domine stared at her. 'I see,' she murmured faintly, glancing round at the group by the door. She realized that Melanie was biased and that there was no love lost between her and her aunt, but in this case she seemed to have a point. Mrs. Mannering had been delighted at the unexpected arrival of their guest, and if James's reaction had been less enthusiastic who could tell what that really meant? She sighed. What did it matter anyway? In six months she would be free of this family and its intrigues for good!

CHAPTER FIVE

MRS. MANNERING insisted that Yvonne joined them for lunch, and during the course of the meal Domine gathered that although Yvonne had an apartment of her own in London, her parents' home was not far from Hollingford, within reach of her father's textile mills at Bradford.

Domine spent the whole meal covertly studying Yvonne's fragile appearance, wondering how James Mannering could fail to be attracted by such perfection. Under the midi coat, Yvonne was wearing a white sheath dress of a woollen material that clung lovingly to the moulded lines of her figure, revealing rather than concealing her obvious attractions. Her hair was a mass of blonde curls, while her complexion was the kind of peaches and cream complexion Domine had read about in magazines, the achievement of which was every Englishwoman's dream. Domine recalled her own olive skin with dislike, and decided with resignation that she would never be able to accomplish such a standard of excellence.

The only jarring note so far as Domine could ascertain was Yvonne's rather shrill speaking voice, which while possessing no trace of an accent nevertheless had none of the huskiness one would have expected. But, Domine reflected philosophically, voices didn't have to be so important, and as Yvonne grew older no doubt her tone would deepen.

When the meal was over, Mrs. Mannering suggested that they all adjourned to the lounge, but James shook his head firmly.

'I told you, Mother, I have some work to do this afternoon,' he averred with just the right amount of polite reluctance in his voice.

Mrs. Mannering compressed her lips irritably. 'Surely you don't intend to neglect your guest by working, James,' she deplored.

James gave a small smile. 'Unfortunately, I have no choice,' he replied, pushing back his chair lazily. 'Besides, Yvonne is well aware of the demands of a writer's life!' Domine thought she sensed a trace of sarcasm in his tone.

Yvonne plucked nervously at a crease in the damask tablecloth. 'I should have thought the amount of work you appear to have been doing at the apartment would have freed you for some time,' she remarked pointedly.

James's smile was not very pleasant, and Domine wondered how Yvonne could stand the barely concealed insolence of his manner.

'Well,' he said, getting to his feet, 'it just shows how mistaken one can be. Now – if you'll all excuse me . . .'

He glanced round the table, his eyes lingering for a moment on Domine's wide-eyed expression, and then he turned and left the room. After he had gone, there was an awful empty silence until Mrs. Mannering said apologetically:

'Oh, Yvonne, I'm so sorry, but you know what James is like when he's working! He's just impossible to live with.'

Yvonne shrugged her slim shoulders, and opening her cigarette case she extracted a long American cigarette and lit it with the attached lighter. Then, after several jerky puffs, she said: 'Well, Geraldine, I don't think there's much point in my hanging around here—'

'That's right!' That was Melanie, leaning back in her chair and regarding Yvonne with deprecatory eyes.

Yvonne chose to ignore her intervention, and went on: 'I did promise to call on the Hamiltons today, too, so I think I'll leave James to his – er – composing!'

'Oh, Yvonne! Must you go?' Mrs. Mannering linked her fingers and unlinked them again. 'I'm sure James doesn't expect you to desert us like that. You could stay and have dinner with us. James will be finished working by then and possibly you two could go for a drive together.'

Yvonne's small teeth caught her lower lip. Then she said: 'Well, I don't know.' She hesitated. 'I don't want to impinge on James's privacy. I know he seeks solitude when he comes to Grey Witches, but as I was passing . . .' She let the sentence trail away. Then she sighed. 'But if you really think he'll be finished by dinner time . . .'

'I'm sure of it!' exclaimed Mrs. Mannering eagerly.

'Then – all right, I'll stay.' Yvonne smiled and relaxed in her chair.

Melanie thrust back her own chair and got to her feet. 'Excuse me,' she said, with exaggerated politeness, and walked out of the room.

Mrs. Mannering smiled after her retreating back and then turned to Yvonne, raising her dark eyebrows expressively. 'Poor Melanie,' she said. 'She does feel at such a disadvantage while you're around, Yvonne!'

Yvonne preened herself under Mrs. Mannering's flattery, and Domine felt that she too had had enough. Rising, she said: 'If you don't want me for anything, Mrs. Mannering, I'll go and take a look around outside.'

Mrs. Mannering studied her for a moment. 'Yes, very well, Domine,' she agreed. 'I'm sure you're quite used to entertaining yourself.'

Domine smiled an assent, and then went out of the dining-room, through the lounge, and into the hall. Only then did she realize she had been holding her breath and expelled it in a long whistle. Thank goodness, she thought, with relief, and collecting her coat she went out of the side door which she, Melanie and James had used that morning.

It was quite chilly, but wonderfully fresh, and buttoning her collar she thrust her hands into her pockets and walked round to the rear of the building where the stables were housed. Now that she had more time to take in her surroundings she could see that there was quite a collection of outbuildings, and a man was swilling out what appeared to be a kind of animal run. There was so sign of Melanie, but as Domine stood there, shivering a little in the wind, the girl appeared from around the corner of the barn carrying a bucket in one hand and a broom in the other.

'Well, well!' she remarked. 'Fancy seeing you here!'

Domine sighed, compressing her lips, and then she walked forward. 'I – I wondered if there was something I could do,' she ventured awkwardly.

Melanie stared at her. 'Are you serious?' Her expression was frankly incredulous.

'Of course I'm serious,' said Domine, nodding. 'Mrs. Mannering explained about the shortage of staff, and I thought I might be able to do something.'

'Is this *her* idea?' asked Melanie suspiciously.

'No, it's mine,' retorted Domine. 'I may look useless, but I can assure you we had to work quite hard at the convent. We weren't run after hand and foot. We had to make our own beds, and keep our rooms tidy, and every week we had to clean out the dining hall and the common room.'

Melanie smiled wryly. 'This is a little different,' she said consideringly. 'Do you mind getting your hands dirty?'

Domine smiled. 'No. In fact, I think I'd rather like it,' she confessed.

Melanie shrugged. 'Well, on your own head be it! But if James grumbles about this, don't say it was my idea!'

'I won't!' agreed Domine, and with a half-friendly laugh, Melanie led the way into the barn.

During the course of the afternoon Domine found that Melanie could be quite an entertaining companion. Her dry wit which had previously been spitefully directed against herself was now pointed towards the tasks they had to tackle, and after Domine had fallen down on the slippery swilled floor of the cowshed, scraped her hands and knees cleaning out the hen-house, and finally inadvertently locked herself in the stall with the bull, they had forgotten their previous antagonism.

It was quite late when Domine left Melanie to lock up, and returned to the house. Going up to her bedroom, she surveyed the picture she made with some amusement. There was straw in her hair, and her hands and face were dirty, while her shoes, which she had carried up the staircase, were thick with mud and manure.

Stripping off, she took a hot bath, then dressed for dinner. She had no time to alter any of her clothes for evening wear and she had to be content with wearing a dark red crêpe skirt that was almost as long as Yvonne's midi coat, and another of her white shirt-blouses. Actually, though, once she was ready it didn't look at all bad, the bright colour suiting her dark complexion.

Her hair depressed her most. The plait was so childish and chunky, and on impulse she undid it and left it loose. But that didn't suit her either. It was too long and it had no style. Rummaging in her drawer, she brought out a red chiffon scarf one of the girls had given her last Christmas and tied her hair back with that, but after a few moments she discarded it also. Then she heard Lily calling that dinner was ready.

With hasty fingers she had to re-plait her hair again, and then run down the stairs because she was so late. They were all seated at the dinner table, everyone that is, but James Mannering. He was not about and Domine could only assume from the tightness of his mother's mouth that they had had another of their confrontations.

'You're late,' Mrs. Mannering said now, sharply, glancing in Yvonne's direction almost sympathetically. Then her expression hardened again, as it rested on Domine. 'You were late for breakfast, and you were late for lunch. Is it too much to expect that you should be on time for a meal?'

'This isn't a hotel, Aunt Geraldine,' Melanie interposed, with sweet sarcasm. 'If you want everyone to toe the line, you'll have to start banging a gong five minutes before the meal is served!'

Mrs. Mannering looked contemptuously at her niece. 'Thank you, Melanie, for your advice, but I don't think a little punctuality is unreasonable, do you, Yvonne?'

Yvonne seemed to be in a bad mood, for all she said was: 'At least unpunctuality is better than complete absence!' in a cold voice.

93

Mrs. Mannering heaved a sigh. 'Yes, I know, and I'm terribly sorry, Yvonne. I wouldn't have asked you to stay if I'd thought—'

Yvonne raised a hand. 'Spare me any more apologies,' she snapped shortly. 'There's absolutely nothing you can say to placate me!' She refused the soup by merely shaking her head at Lily as she made to ladle some on to her plate. 'To think I could have been dining with the Hamiltons! I'm sure Gerald Hamilton wouldn't expect a guest of his to accept being ignored for the whole day!'

Melanie grimaced at Domine, and Domine tried not to smile. But it was a warming feeling to realize that this day that had started so badly had ended with her feeling so much less of an outsider. Now it was Yvonne who was the odd one out, and she didn't like it. Domine wondered what James was doing. Had he gone out? Or was he simply not having dinner?

'Just imagine!' exclaimed Yvonne petulantly. 'He actually asked for a tray in his room! If he has to eat, why can't he eat with us?'

Melanie shrugged. 'You're too much of a distraction, Yvonne,' she murmured mockingly, and Domine choked over her soup and had to have Melanie thump her on the back.

Yvonne left immediately after dinner, driving away recklessly in the red low-slung sports car that had brought her to Grey Witches. Mrs. Mannering retired to bed with a headache and as Melanie was engrossed in a book about horse-breeding, Domine watched television. It was quite a novelty really and she enjoyed it. She refused Lily's offer of supper and went to bed early feeling a little less alien than the previous night . . .

During the next few days she saw little of James

Mannering. According to his mother he was continually on the telephone to London and she abhorred the bills he must be running up. She had by no means got over the way he had acted the day Yvonne Park had spent with them, but if her constrained attitude was an attempt to bring pressure to bear on her son she didn't seem to be making much progress.

Domine's days were full of riding and walking and helping Melanie. The older girl seemed to have accepted her for what she was, and obviously didn't consider she represented any problems so far as James Mannering was concerned. As they got to know one another, Melanie had confided her affection for James, and had admitted that he was the only reason she put up with Geraldine Mannering's barbs, but although Domine appreciated Melanie's trust she couldn't dispel the disturbing emotions that the other girl's words had aroused in her. Maybe it was because for the first time in nine years she was living a normal, family life that Domine felt such an unreasonably possessive attitude towards her guardian, she didn't know, but she did know that she didn't want him to consider marrying anybody right now.

The weather maintained a calm countenance and the mornings were becoming quite frosty. Domine always rose early and went out with Rosie, the mare, on to the moors. Sometimes Melanie accompanied her, and once James himself joined them, but mostly she was alone and she forgot the anger James had displayed that first morning when she had ridden away on her own. After all, she was never too far from the house, and she felt quite capable of avoiding any unsavoury characters she might encounter.

All the same, she got quite a start one morning when she had dismounted and was allowing Rosie to crop the grass and a horseman came galloping up to her. Gathering the mare's reins ready to make her escape, she relaxed smilingly when she saw that the horseman was none other than Vincent Morley.

'Hello there!' he said cheerfully. 'This is a pleasant surprise.'

Domine smiled, and allowed Rosie to go on cropping the turf.

'I've not seen you on the moors before,' she said, looking up.

Vincent dismounted. 'You mean you do this regularly?'

Domine nodded. 'Most mornings.'

'I see.' Vincent's smile warmed her. 'I must make a point of riding out more often. Where do you usually go?'

'Oh, just about this far,' said Domine, looking round. 'Just so that I can see the sea. It's a lovely view from here.'

'Have you been down to the coast? To Whitby or Scarborough?'

Domine shook her head. 'No. Actually, I haven't been anywhere yet. Mr. Mannering is busy writing, and I've been helping Melanie about the farm.'

'Good heavens!' Vincent Morley frowned. 'But surely your guardian doesn't know you're doing that!'

Domine shrugged. 'I don't know whether he knows or not. Does it matter?'

'Well, I should say so. After all, there's no necessity for it.'

'I know, but I enjoy it,' said Domine simply. She sighed. 'It is beautiful here, isn't it? I never get tired of the emptiness of it all.'

Vincent shook his head. 'You're an unusual girl,' he

remarked. 'Most girls in your position and with your opportunities would be hankering after the bright lights. I should have thought James would have found it difficult to keep you here.'

Domine bent her head. 'I suppose it's easier for him – keeping me here, I mean, and as he happens to be able to work at the moment, I don't think he notices either me or his surroundings.'

Vincent took out some cigarettes and offered her one and they smoked companionably for a few minutes. Then Vincent said:

'Anyway, you'll be leaving for London soon enough, I suppose. This play of James's, the one they're performing on television, it's to be screened in a few days, isn't it?'

Domine frowned. 'Is it? Oh! I didn't know.' She swept back the fringe from her brow. 'Do you think James will need to go back for that?' His name came naturally to her and she didn't attempt to retract it.

Vincent frowned. 'Well, I would think so. It's usual for last-minute directing and so on.'

Domine's heart fluttered a little. 'I see. I shall be sorry to go.'

And yet would she? she thought with candour. Yorkshire appealed to her most strongly because she had found a home here, but without James Mannering the home would be incomplete even if his remarks to her were few and far between. He was there – and that was the important thing.

Suddenly and almost simultaneously, they heard the sound of horse's hooves and Domine shaded her eyes to see who was approaching them. When she recognized her guardian, the fluttering in her breast increased uncomfortably. He was scowling when he reached them, and he sat astride the black hunter regarding them sourly.

'So this is where you've got to,' he said, addressing Domine, harshly. 'Melanie told me you were out alone.'

'I am – at least, I was,' Domine amended hastily. 'Mr. Morley just encountered me a few minutes ago.'

'Indeed?' James looked dourly at Vincent. 'I didn't know you rode out here in the mornings.'

'I don't very often,' replied Vincent calmly. 'It was by sheer chance I came up on Miss Grainger.'

James considered this and then said: 'Are you ready to ride back, Domine?' in a cold tone.

Domine gathered the mare's reins, stepping on the stub of her cigarette. 'Yes, I'm ready,' she agreed, climbing into the saddle.

'Then I'll say goodbye – for now,' said Vincent, smiling rather sardonically. 'I may see you again some morning, Miss Grainger.'

Domine nodded and smiled, and then Vincent Morley wheeled his horse and rode off with a casual salute. After he had gone, Domine made as if to move away, but James leant across and caught the reins, preventing her from controlling her mount.

'I want to talk to you,' he said bleakly, 'and now is as good a time as any.'

Domine shivered. 'I'm cold,' she said, rather nervously. 'Can't we talk back at the house?'

'No. There are too many distractions there. Besides, my mother is careful to see we're never left completely alone together.'

Domine flushed. 'I can't imagine why,' she exclaimed.

'Can't you?' He gave a harsh smile. 'Then obviously

you haven't been looking at yourself lately. With good food inside you, and plenty of fresh air and exercise, you're developing into an attractive girl.'

'Why, thank you,' she murmured, attempting a casual tone and failing dismally.

James glanced round, then he said: 'Follow me,' and allowed his horse to canter away across the moor. Domine followed him, glancing round occasionally to keep her bearings, for this was all new territory to her. Presently she saw James's objective. Ahead of them was a shepherd's hut, the kind of shed-like dwelling that could be used as a place for making a hot drink by a farmer searching for lambs or lost sheep.

Reaching the hut, James dismounted and tethered his horse outside, then waited for Domine to join him. However, she dismounted swiftly, avoiding his assistance, and when he pushed open the door she preceded him into the hut. It was a stark lodging with only a bench and a table, and a spirit stove in one corner. But at least it was warmer out of the frosty morning air, and the light that filtered through the dusty window was already tinged with sunlight.

Domine moved round the table, putting some little space between herself and her guardian, then said, 'Now what do you want to say? That we're leaving for London in a day or so?'

James frowned. 'Now where did you hear that?'

'Mr. Morley was just telling me,' she replied, shrugging. 'He told me that your play is going to be transmitted in a few days' time.'

'That's right, it is,' said James, kicking at the unoffending leg of the table with his boot. 'As my mother has constantly been complaining, I've been on the phone to London most days, but even so, it's still become necessary for me to go down. Besides, it's better to be on the spot.'

'I can understand that,' nodded Domine.

'The point is – I don't want you to come with me,' he continued quietly.

Domine's head jerked up. 'What?'

He sighed. 'You heard what I said, Domine. I want you to stay here – at Grey Witches.'

'But why?' Domine felt indignant. 'You were the one who insisted I remained here with you, even though my great-uncle made no provision for me. Now you say you're going back to London, and leaving me behind! Was that your intention all along? To bring me here and abandon me?'

James chewed his lip. 'I'm not abandoning you, Domine,' he exclaimed impatiently. 'You know you couldn't possibly stay with me at the apartment in town!'

'Why not?'

'Don't be deliberately obtuse! I don't need to spell it out for you, do I? God, in no time at all people would be saying we were living together.'

'Well, we would be,' she said moodily.

'All right, then,' he snapped, 'sleeping together!'

Domine's cheeks suffused with colour. 'As you consider me such a child, there'd be no question of that!' she retorted painfully.

James glared at her. 'I am not treating you as a child, Domine. Hell, it's not many minutes ago that I agreed you were an attractive girl—'

'How kind!' Domine's eyes flashed. 'How *patronizing*!'

'Oh, what's got into you, Domine?' he exclaimed, raking a hand through his thick hair. 'What do you want me to say? I don't know the current teenage jargon!'

'And nor do I!' she returned fiercely. 'My regular escort was a man in his seventies, remember?' She twisted her fingers together. 'At least he treated me as his equal!'

'Very appropriate!' remarked James cruelly. 'He was in his second childhood!'

Domine's face mirrored the hurt he had so carelessly inflicted. 'Why do you say that?' she cried. 'Because he was decent enough to care for an orphaned girl, giving her someone to care about and to care about her!'

James shook his head rather contritely. 'No, I didn't mean that,' he said patiently. 'You're deliberately misunderstanding me. Look, I'm sorry about this, but there's nothing I can do!'

Domine sniffed. 'Isn't there?' she asked miserably.

James came round the table to her side, placing his hands on her shoulders as he had done once before. 'Look, Domine, I don't want to hurt you,' he began. 'Heavens, I've known what it's like to feel lost and lonely. But that's not for you!' He shook her gently. 'I shan't be gone for ever. I'll be back almost before you've noticed I've gone.'

Domine looked up at him. 'And will you bring me a nice teddy bear to take to bed with me?' she asked mockingly, hiding her fears in baiting him.

His fingers tightened on her shoulders. 'You deserve a good hiding for that!' he snapped angrily.

'And who'll administer it, you?' she taunted him, unable to prevent herself.

'If necessary, yes,' he muttered violently. 'And don't get any ideas about disappearing in my absence, because if you do I'll find you, make no mistake about that!'

Domine wrenched herself out of his grip and turned away, fingering her braid of hair. 'Oh, go away now, for all I care,' she exclaimed, unwillingly aware that she was near to tears. She stared through the grimy window of the hut out on to the wild expanses of the moor and thought its desolation was symbolic of the desperation she was feeling. She had grown to love the bleakness of it all, but in spite of that she could not bear the idea of James returning to London and leaving her here. After all, Christmas was only about five weeks away and he might not return until then. She hunched her shoulders. Maybe even then it was a doubtful possibility. These were hardly the kind of surroundings he would choose in which to celebrate the festive season. He was rich, comparatively young, attractive to women; his sophisticated tastes had been denied long enough. She might not get the chance to spend any time with him again. Once Christmas was over, her six months would soon be up. The knowledge made her reckless. Without looking at him, she said: 'You can't stop me coming to London on my own!'

James uttered an expletive. 'You're to stay here, Domine,' he commanded furiously. 'Hell, I won't be dictated to like this!'

Domine swung round. 'And nor will I,' she retorted angrily. 'You took me away from everything I'd ever known – you opened Pandora's box and set me free – well, see if you can control me now!' and without another word she wrenched open the door of the hut and stormed out into the icy morning air.

Running to the mare, she grasped the reins and swung herself into the saddle as he appeared in the doorway of the hut. Giving him a scornful glance, she dug her heels into the animal's side and set her cantering away across the moor. But cantering wasn't absorbing enough, her mind could still torture itself with thoughts, and she leant low, urging the horse on, pressing it into a gallop. She was uncaring of anything just at that moment, but a desire to escape from the despair that enveloped her.

The wind tore at her sweater, lifted her fringe and loosened tendrils of hair from the braid, ran its freezing fingers down her spine. But there was exhilaration in fighting its force, a numbing sense of achievement in racing into its blast. The mare's breath mingled with her own as steam in the frosty air, and Domine gave her her head.

Unfortunately she had not considered which direction she was taking and the roughness of the earth underfoot warned her that this was new ground she was covering, ground that could be dangerously riddled with rabbit-holes or air-vents to the underground workings of years gone by. Rosie stumbled once, and Domine managed to right her, drawing on the mare's bit, trying to prevent her headlong passage into what could be disaster. But Rosie was enjoying herself too much, and she refused to accept the attempt at restriction. Instead she surged on with Domine clinging to her back until she finally responded to control and came cantering to a standstill. Domine was sweating from the exertion, and trembling from the realization that she had unwittingly endangered the mare's life. Sliding from her back, she patted her steaming flesh, taking deep breaths and trying to dispel the awful feeling of panic that the mare's bolt had aroused in her.

And even as she stood there, she heard the hooves of James Mannering's hunter thundering down upon her, and presently he reached her, swinging from the saddle to grasp her and shake her furiously.

'You crazy little idiot!' he swore violently. 'Have you no sense at all? Don't you know Rosie could have stumbled and you could have been thrown? What's got into you, Domine? Are you deliberately trying to prove that you're not safe to be left alone? Is that it?'

Domine felt unutterably weary. Putting up a hand, she swept back her tangled hair from her eyes, and stared at him without defiance. There was nothing more to be said. No matter how she tried, she was no match for his strength. Yet even as she stared at him she realized that his eyes were no longer cold and enigmatic, but burning with a passionate anger that gave a flame-like brilliance to the blueness.

'Well?' he muttered harshly. 'Haven't you anything to say for yourself? Or are you still shaken, too?'

Domine shook her head without speaking, and he closed his eyes for a moment as though to shut out the sight of her. Then he heaved a sigh, and said: 'You could have killed yourself!' in a curiously uneven voice.

Domine swallowed hard. 'I – I know, I know,' she said tremulously. 'I'm sorry if I disturbed you—'

'Disturbed me!' he echoed, a trifle thickly. 'What an inadequate word!' His fingers slid across her shoulders to her throat, cupping its slenderness but not savagely. He shook his head exasperatedly. 'What am I going to do with you?'

Domine shivered even though she was not cold and a new awareness of him gripped her. No matter what he thought, she was not the child he had imagined he was going to be responsible for. She was a young woman, with a woman's needs, and foolishly she was allowing herself to drift into a situation where he was becoming important to her, much more important than any guardian could ever be. She wasn't quite sure how she knew this, certainly she was not experienced in that direction, but some things were instinctive, and this was one of them.

In consequence, she thrust such ridiculous longings aside, and said quite coolly: 'I'm cold. I want to go back to the house.'

He set her free instantly, and turned to his horse, mounting without another word, and wheeling the animal towards Grey Witches. 'Follow me!' he commanded, and cantered away.

Domine found it difficult to mount at all considering she was shaking quite badly now, and not only with the cold. But at last she managed to climb on to Rosie's back and allowed her to follow the hunter home. By the time they reached the stables. she was numb with cold, but blowing on her hands she unsaddled the mare and began to rub her down herself She had thought James had gone into the house, leaving the hunter to one of the men. but presently he emerged from the stables, and when he saw Domine busily engaged in her task, he said. rather bleakly:

'Leave it! Go indoors. You're blue with cold.'

Domine hesitated. and then decided not to argue. Instead, she nodded and went through the entrance into the hall. She wished she had more courage to stand up to him This morning's effort had exhausted her both physically and mentally, and she went up to her room with a heavy heart.

CHAPTER SIX

For the rest of the day James was closeted in his study, and although Domine attended meals, he did not. Neither Mrs. Mannering nor Melanie saw anything strange in that. He very often was absent for meals. But after supper, when the three women were sitting in the lounge together, Mrs. Mannering said:

'James leaves for London tomorrow. Did you know, Melanie?'

Melanie shrugged. 'No, but then nobody bothers to tell me anything,' she replied good-humouredly. She glanced at Domine who was flicking through the pages of a magazine. 'What about Domine?'

Mrs. Mannering raised her dark eyebrows. 'She'll stay here, of course.'

Melanie grimaced. 'There's no "of course" about it, Aunt Geraldine. You know James. He's just as likely to decide he's going to take her with him.'

Mrs. Mannering controlled her annoyance. 'I happen to know that Domine *is* staying here,' she said tightly. 'Will you pass me a cigarette, Domine, my dear?'

Domine got up to hand Mrs. Mannering the cigarette box from an occasional table, and then waited to light her cigarette with the table lighter. 'Thank you,' Mrs. Mannering smiled pleasantly and blew smoke into the air. 'Have you ever smoked, Domine?'

Domine shrugged, and resumed her seat. 'Occasionally,' she admitted. 'It had to be done in secret, of course. The Sisters at the convent, naturally, didn't approve of nicotine.'

'Naturally,' echoed Mrs. Mannering. 'Tell me, why do you suppose Henry took you away from the orphanage?'

Melanie looked a trifle impatiently in her aunt's direction. 'Is that relevant, Aunt Geraldine?' she questioned, rather shortly. Of late she had taken to sticking up for Domine.

'I think it's perfectly relevant,' replied Mrs. Mannering, with obvious annoyance. 'Well, Domine?'

Domine sighed, and closed the magazine. 'I don't know,' she said, pensively, resting her head against the back of the chair. 'I suppose because I was my father's child. My father was his nephew.'

'Yes, I am aware of the relationship,' remarked Mrs. Mannering sardonically. 'However, I don't believe that Henry had shown any particular interest in your family before this – unhappy – time, had he?'

Domine flushed. 'Not particularly. We – we did get Christmas cards – that sort of thing.'

'Yes – but it was strange, was it not, that after so many years of – well, separation, he should suddenly decide to make you his ward.'

'My parents had just been killed,' Domine pointed out, rather tautly. 'Until then I don't suppose he thought we – well, needed him.'

Mrs. Mannering shook her head. 'I simply cannot fathom his motives.'

'Did he have to have any?' asked Domine quietly.

'Oh, yes!' Mrs. Mannering gave a short laugh. 'If you'd known Henry Farriday as well as I knew Henry Farriday, you wouldn't ask that question.'

Melanie looked at Domine's rather exhausted young face, and said: 'Maybe, dear aunt, your persistent attempts to torment him drove him away.' She smiled mockingly. 'Just as they're driving James away now.'

'Be quiet!' Mrs. Mannering's annoyance erupted into anger. 'James has a perfectly legitimate reason for going to London!'

'Has he?' Melanie looked sceptical. 'Or is he aware that if he emerges from the seclusion of his study here, you'll have Yvonne here so fast her feet won't touch the ground?'

'How dare you speak to me like this?' gasped Mrs. Mannering furiously. 'Melanie, apologize!'

Melanie lay back in her chair, folding her legs. 'Okay, okay,' she said, a trifle resignedly. 'Maybe that was going a bit too far. But I still maintain, people don't want to be manoeuvred all their lives.'

'No one manoeuvred Henry Farriday,' exclaimed Mrs. Mannering, trying to gather her composure.

'Agreed. So maybe I was right. Maybe he found a respite from your badgering with Domine,' asserted Melanie.

Domine sighed. Mrs. Mannering and Melanie were constantly antagonistic towards one another, and James was the usual subject of contention. Melanie was right when she averred that Mrs. Mannering was ambitious for her son in every direction.

'Well, anyway,' said Mrs. Mannering, 'I wish I could be certain that Henry had not some trump card up his sleeve, just waiting to be played.'

'What trump card could he have?' Domine was curious.

Melanie shrugged. 'Who knows?' She smiled at Domine. 'My aunt has the apprehensions of the guilt-stricken!'

'Melanie!' Mrs. Mannering stubbed out her cigarette angrily. 'I will not listen to your ridiculous baiting! If you can't keep your opinions to yourself, then kindly go to your room!'

Melanie didn't move, but she lifted the magazine Domine had discarded and began to glance at it indifferently. Domine felt uncomfortable. It was bad enough sitting here pretending she didn't care that James was leaving in the morning without listening to the two women fencing with each other.

Sighing, she got to her feet, and Mrs. Mannering looked up. 'Where are you going, Domine?'

'To my room.'

'Why? Are you tired of Melanie's rudeness, too?'

Domine coloured. 'I'm tired,' she said, refusing to enter the argument, and Melanie half-smiled to herself. Then the door opened, and James came into the room.

Dressed in cream slacks and a dark sweater, he looked dark and attractive, and Domine felt her heart contract in a most peculiar way. He looked across at her flushed cheeks and said, rather wearily:

'What's going on? I heard raised voices.'

Melanie looked up resignedly. 'Your mother has been laying down her law again,' she replied sardonically, 'and I think your ward has had just about enough.'

Mrs. Mannering rose to her feet. 'James, have I to suffer Melanie's rudeness indefinitely, or are you going to ask her to leave?'

James heaved a sigh. 'You know very well that without Melanie Grey Witches would fall apart,' he said honestly. 'You make a good mistress, Mother, but you seem to have forgotten the practical necessities of living. Without Melanie's help you would find your life much different.'

'James!'

'Well, it's true.' He thrust his hands into his

pockets. 'Anyway, Domine won't have to put up with your bickering after tonight. I'm taking her with me tomorrow.'

Domine's heart somersaulted sickly, and she had to put out a hand to support herself on the back of a chair. He couldn't be serious. He was actually telling his mother he was taking her to London!

Mrs. Mannering's mouth tightened. 'That's impossible, James, and you know it. The girl can't possibly live with you at the apartment.'

'Why not?'

Mrs. Mannering pressed a hand to her throat. 'You – ask me – that!' she exclaimed. 'Oh, James, don't talk so foolishly! Domine is staying here. Besides,' she hesitated, 'besides, Melanie needs her help. She's proved quite useful about the farm, hasn't she, Melanie?'

Melanie gave an indifferent shrug, and Domine realized that the older girl liked this no more than Mrs. Mannering did, but that she was keeping her thoughts to herself. It was Melanie's attitude that caused Domine to say, quite clearly:

'Don't alarm yourself unnecessarily, Mrs. Mannering. I shall not be going with your son. I – I would prefer to stay here!'

James's eyes burned into hers, and he said tautly: 'That's not the whole truth, Domine.'

Domine straightened her shoulders. 'Isn't it?' She managed a light smile. 'Of course it is.' She saw the relief in Melanie's face and pressed on: 'Besides, your work is in London, and I should only be in the way.'

Mrs. Mannering nodded enthusiastically. 'Yes, that's right, James,' she said, crossing the room and taking his arm.

James shook her off and looked piercingly at Domine. 'You *want* to stay here?' he asked coldly.

Domine shivered. She wanted to say *no*, that she wanted to leave with him more than anything else in the world, but that would be ridiculous and traitorous when she knew how much Melanie thought of him. And besides, he was only asking her to go because of the situation here, because he thought she might run away after he had left and he didn't want her on his conscience. He had no real desire for her company; what possible pleasure could he get out of her company anyway? He was so much older, so much more experienced, while she was merely a nuisance, an oddity, a responsibility.

'Yes,' she said now. 'I want to stay.'

He studied her for another disturbing moment, and then he shrugged. 'So be it!' he remarked wryly, and with an indifferent gesture he left the room.

As soon as James had left for London Domine regretted the impulse that had made her refuse to go with him. The whole day she imagined him driving down through the November mists, and there was an awful tugging feeling in her heart. But deciding that physical exercise was the best medicine for the blues, she joined Melanie in the stables and worked until her whole body ached and all she longed to do was climb into bed.

During the days that followed she used the same method to dispel her melancholy, and eventually the resilience of youth returned, and she began to wonder when he would return. The night his play was performed on television, Mrs. Mannering had dinner served early so that they could all watch it, and Domine was pleasantly surprised to discover it was quite a straightforward production with a real story, and not one of those awful presentations where the viewer was left high and dry at the end, wondering what he had actually witnessed.

When it was over, Mrs. Mannering went into the hall to telephone her son and offer her congratulations at the success the play had been, and Domine and Melanie went into the kitchen to prepare supper.

Pouring milk into cups, Melanie said wryly: 'Aunt Geraldine has made sure her congratulations will be offered in a personal way. She arranged for Yvonne to be admitted to the producer's box during the transmission.'

Domine quelled the feeling of dismay this aroused inside her. 'Isn't that rather futile?' she asked casually. 'I mean – it's obvious that James isn't interested in Yvonne.'

Melanie shrugged. 'There is such a thing as habit, you know,' she said dryly. 'Aunt Geraldine thinks that if she keeps throwing them together James will get used to the idea of having Yvonne around. A few months ago she thought she had succeeded. James spent a lot of time with our poor little rich girl. But nothing seems to last with him. He soon tires of these brainless beauties. Basically, he's a Yorkshireman at heart, and there's a hard streak in him that demands something more than mere good looks and social position. Besides, think what an uninteresting existence it would be with someone like Yvonne whose main interests are having a good time and clothes! Or should I say clothes and having a good time? I think they vie with each other for first position.' She gave a harsh laugh. 'I used to think James would marry me some day.' She shrugged. 'I'm beginning to realize that's a vain hope, too. I sometimes wonder if he'll ever marry anyone. Although he likes women – at least,' she gave Domine a wry glance, 'he needs a woman, now and then, he's not as sensual as a man in his position could be.' She sighed and leant back against the stainless steel draining board. 'Tell me, Domine, how do you see him?'

Domine shrugged, turning away to take a tin of biscuits out of the cupboard so that Melanie should not see her expression. 'He's really very kind,' she said at last. 'I mean – it was kind, wasn't it, taking on the responsibility for me?'

Melanie nodded. 'Oh, yes, he's kind. And he's gentle sometimes. He has a foul temper, and I've seen him thrash a man when the other fellow criticized his mother, but he has charm, and with charm one can get away with murder.' She smoothed the cool steel of the sink thoughtfully. 'Why didn't you go with him – to London?' Her eyes when she turned them on Domine were searching.

Domine bent her head. 'I – I don't know,' she confessed. 'Why?'

Melanie grimaced. 'Oh, kid, don't go falling for him,' she exclaimed. 'I know the signs – I've been there myself!'

Domine looked up. 'I'm not a kid, you know,' she said, with dignity.

Melanie smiled. 'Aren't you? Well, maybe not, but to James Mannering you are. Heavens, he's old enough to be your father, do you know that?'

'Not quite,' said Domine tightly.

'Oh, yes, quite,' retorted Melanie. 'He's thirty-seven, you're seventeen! At twenty, James was quite capable of fathering you!'

Domine flushed. 'I'm almost eighteen,' she pointed out quietly. Then she brushed back her fringe with her hand. 'In any case, this is a purely senseless discussion. I have no intention of "falling for" James, and certainly there's no fear of him falling for me!'

Melanie considered this. 'No, I would agree with you up to a point. My only anxiety where you're concerned is that you could get hurt. I'm not sure how or why, but I feel it.'

'Oh, don't be silly!' cried Domine. 'Look, the percolater's bubbling!'

Melanie unplugged the coffee pot and placed it on the trolley she was preparing to take into the lounge, then looked at Domine thoughtfully. 'You're an attractive creature, Domine,' she said quietly. 'You weren't when you came, wet and miserable, and lost somehow. But now, after three weeks of good food and country air, you're a different proposition, and I'm just afraid that—' She bit her lip and shook her head. 'Don't let James hurt you,' she said briefly, and without another word she wheeled the trolley through to the lounge.

Domine frowned. She could have told Melanie she was a little late with her warning. James had already hurt her.

During the second week after James's departure, when Domine was beginning to feel low again, Vincent Morley called one morning and asked whether he might be allowed to take her to Scarborough with him. His mother lived there, apparently, and he was going to visit her and thought Domine might enjoy the opportunity of seeing the countryside and the town itself.

Mrs. Mannering was quite amiable, and although Domine felt guilty at leaving Melanie with everything to do alone, the older girl gently urged her to accept Vincent's invitation.

'He's a nice young man,' she said, smiling in her sardonic way. 'Much more suitable for you than cleaning out the henhouses.'

Domine chuckled, but it was quite exciting getting ready and wondering whether she might spend some of her money on some new clothes and perhaps a few oddments for Christmas, which was fast approaching.

In the event, she enjoyed the day enormously. Vincent was a good companion, and she discovered quite a lot about him. They left immediately after lunch, and as it was one of those crisp November days when the air tasted like wine, Domine relaxed in the Land-Rover feeling quite different from the shy creature she had been when she drove away from the convent with James. At least living with Mrs. Mannering and Melanie had taught her to stand up for herself.

When they arrived in Scarborough, they wandered round the shops for a while, and Domine was amazed at the amount of boutiques there were, all with clothes suitable for teenagers and young women. She chose a red coat for herself in the new midi length, and while it was not as richly-textured as Yvonne's had been, it suited her olive colouring. To wear with it she bought a dress of royal blue jersey that clung in all the right places, and finally some knee-length leather boots, and some gloves and a handbag to match. She put all her purchases in the back of the Land-Rover and then they drove down to the promenade so that Domine could see the shoreline. But they did not linger. Everywhere was closed for the season and there was a melancholy air about shuttered windows and sheeted amusements.

Finally they drove towards Peasholm Park on the north side of the town where Mrs. Morley lived in a rather attractive bungalow. She was a widow and she welcomed them warmly, making Domine feel quite at home. Not much older than Mrs. Mannering, she had none of the other woman's hardness, and there was genuine regret in her voice when, after a delicious high tea of ham and pineapple, fruit trifle and home-made cakes, they had to leave.

'You must come again,' she averred, smiling at her son. 'Vincent will bring you, won't you, love?'

Vincent nodded enthusiastically. 'Of course. This is Domine's first visit to Scarborough. She must come when everything starts moving again, and the sun is really warm.'

'Yes, that's right,' said Mrs. Morley, nodding, 'but don't wait that long to bring her, will you?' She chuckled.

In the Land-Rover, going home, Domine said: 'Oh, your mother is nice, isn't she? I think she's exactly the way a mother should be.'

Vincent smiled. 'She liked you, too. I think she considers I'm becoming set in my ways, and when I produce a girl for her inspection she immediately jumps to conclusions.'

Domine coloured in the darkness, and he continued: 'Not that I've brought many girls to meet her. She's not the kind to take to some of these so-called "swingers".' He smiled wryly. 'And I know I'm getting less attached to the solitude of my house. Oh, I have a woman who comes in and keeps the place clean, but it's not much fun cooking just for one.'

Domine bit her lip. She had the feeling that while he might protest, Vincent was allowing his mother's attitude towards him settling down to influence his relationships with girls. No girl wanted to be taken too seriously too soon. It was a little like rushing things. So Domine changed the subject, and stared out into the darkness, wondering with a pang where James Mannering was tonight. There had been no word from him for her, although Mrs. Mannering had spoken to him once or twice on the telephone. Melanie had confided to her that Mrs. Mannering's plans could not be bearing fruit yet or they would have heard about it, and in a gossip column Melanie had read that James had been seen in the company of Lucia Marcinello, the widow of an Italian ship-owner, whose organization had gone bankrupt, causing him to decide he had nothing left to live for. 'Naturally, that won't please Aunt Geraldine,' Melanie had remarked wryly. 'Apart from the obvious lack of funds, the tragedy caused quite a scandal a couple of months ago.' Domine had had no opinion to offer, and had, instead, spent a sleepless night trying to decide what best she could do when her six months with the Mannerings was over.

Vincent left her at the entrance to Grey Witches, taking her hand enthusiastically and thus avoiding the awkwardness of a first kiss. 'You will come out with me again, won't you, Domine?' he asked.

Domine nodded. 'If you want me to. Thank you for taking me to meet your mother. I did enjoy it. And you've been very understanding, wasting time in dress shops and shoe shops, and so on.' She smiled apologetically, accepting the parcels from him.

'It was a pleasure,' exclaimed Vincent eagerly. 'Well, I'll say good-bye, then.'

'Yes.' Domine turned to the door. 'Good-bye, Vincent.'

Vincent hesitated, looked as though he would have liked to have kissed her, and then hastened down the steps to the Land-Rover, raising a hand as Domine pushed open the heavy door and entered the hall and was temporarily illuminated in the light emanating from inside the house.

During the next week, Domine went out with Vincent three times. He took her to the cinema, to a meeting of motor-cycle scrambling enthusiasts, and once out to dinner to a roadhouse near York. On the latter occasion, Domine wore her new dress and coat, together with the accessories including the long black boots. She was amazed at the difference the modern clothes made to her appearance, and during the afternoon Melanie, who she had found was quite an adept at such things, cut and styled her hair, shortening it to just above her shoulders and giving the ends an upward tilt.

When Vincent came to call for her she was gratified by the eager light in his eyes, and the way he helped her gallantly into the Land-Rover. 'I suppose you really ought to be driving in a super sports car,' he murmured regretfully, 'but as I get this vehicle provided for my estate work, I didn't see much point in wasting money on another car.'

Domine smiled mischievously at him. 'You don't have to explain yourself to me,' she said. 'I don't mind.'

Vincent touched her hand for a moment. 'I think you're adorable,' he said honestly. 'Tonight – I don't know!' He shook his head. 'You look altogether different. It's those clothes. The bright colours suit your colouring.'

'Thank you, Vincent,' she said demurely, and felt a sense of contentment assail her. Vincent was always so nice, so pleasant, so sweet. She was amazed that some girl hadn't snapped him up before this. After all, he would be very easy to love.

And yet would he? argued a voice inside her. Wasn't he just a little too easy-going? Life with him might be dull – very dull! She wrinkled her nose. Anyway, it was nothing to do with her. Whatever his thoughts might be in the matter, their relationship remained that of friends and nothing more, and that was how Domine intended it should stay. After all, in less than four months she would be leaving here for good, and she might never see him again.

The roadhouse was neon-lighted, and expensive, and the meal they enjoyed surpassed anything Domine had previously experienced, except perhaps for the dinner Graham had prepared for herself and James Mannering that night at the apartment. When it was over, he taught her to move with him round the dance-floor, it could not be called dancing, and she laughed a lot and relaxed completely.

Afterwards they drove back to Grey Witches across the moonlit moors, and Domine thought she had never seen them look so beautiful. It was a marvellous evening, cold and frosty, but brilliant, and the stars seemed brighter than usual. Hollingford was mostly in darkness, many of the villagers who rose early to attend to their chores went to bed early, but there were plenty of lights at Grey Witches, and as they turned into the drive Domine saw a familiar car parked at the entrance. Immediately her heart began to thump uncomfortably, and Vincent said: 'That's James's car, isn't it?'

Domine nodded. 'I think so. I didn't know he was coming back.'

Vincent gave a wry smile. 'When does anyone know anything about James Mannering?' he asked dryly. 'Does it bother you? That you were out when he arrived?'

Domine swallowed hard, straightening her shoulders. 'Heavens, no!' she denied quickly. 'Besides, what I do is nothing to do with him.'

Vincent raised his eyebrows. 'I should have thought he wouldn't agree with you there,' he remarked. 'You are his responsibility after all, and it's late, later than I expected, actually.'

Domine sighed. 'I'm not a child, Vincent.'

'Agreed. Point taken.' He smiled. 'Do you want my support when you go in?'

Domine shook her head. 'No, that won't be necessary, Vincent. In fact, I think it would be as well if you didn't. If James has just driven up from London he'll be in no mood for visitors.'

'That's right.' Vincent nodded, bringing the Land-Rover to a halt near James's car. 'In any case, I shall have to call and see him tomorrow. I always call when he's here to let him know everything that's going on.'

Domine nodded, and slid out of her seat, leaning in at the window. 'Okay,' she said. 'Don't bother to get out. I can mount the steps without encountering any pitfalls, I think. See you tomorrow, Vincent?'

'Sure thing!' Vincent was eager. 'Good-bye.'

As he drove away, Domine mounted the steps and entered the house through the heavy front door. Closing it, she realized all the hall lights were on, and strewn all over the hall floor were grey suitcases. Frowning, she shook her head. This couldn't all be James's luggage He must have brought someone with him. Even as this thought crossed her mind, she heard a sound, and looking up she encountered James's eyes as he stood watching her from the door of the lounge. He was surveying her rather appraisingly, and she felt a ridiculous sense of pleasure that she was looking her best. Certainly the new clothes and the new hairstyle added years to her appearance, and she no longer looked like the schoolgirl he had collected from the convent.

'What have you been doing until this hour?' he asked, and she realized that he was furiously angry. His voice was cold and there was an ominous glint in those blue eyes, now like chips of an iceberg.

Domine recovered from the sense of disappointment she had experienced at being treated so harshly the moment she returned to the house, and said lightly: 'Didn't your mother tell you where I was?'

James came fully into the hall. In a dark suit, his hair slightly tousled as though he had been raking his hands through it, he looked disturbingly attractive, but she almost took a step backwards at his expression. 'Yes, she told me,' he snapped violently. 'But it's now almost midnight. And I didn't ask where you'd been, I asked what you'd been doing.'

Domine stiffened. 'We've been driving home from York,' she retorted, a coolness creeping into her own tones. 'It does take quite some time, you know. And I wasn't aware that there was any curfew tonight!'

'Don't be insolent,' he bit out coldly. 'Even my mother was concerned about you.'

Domine hunched her shoulders. It didn't matter that this was the first time she had been so late, or that Vincent himself had regretted leaving it so late to return home, she objected to his heavy-handed method of handling the situation. On top of which, her appearance obviously gave him no pleasure from the way he was scowling at her.

'Is that all?' she asked now, uncaring of whoever it was he had brought with him. Her curiosity had dissipated with her happiness.

'No, it is not all, damn you,' he muttered fiercely. 'What have you been doing to yourself?'

Domine looked mutinous. 'You said I needed taking in hand, remember?' she taunted him.

James clenched his fists, and then thrust his hands into the pockets of his trousers. 'And who cut your hair?' he inquired harshly.

Domine sighed. 'Melanie. And she didn't actually cut it. She trimmed it, that's all. For heaven's sake, I thought you'd be pleased that I don't look such a frump as I did when you went away!'

'You never looked a frump,' he asserted moodily. 'Are those clothes new, too?'

'Yes!' Domine was past trying to humour him. 'I'm sure you consider them bad taste, don't you? Well, I don't! I like them. And so does Vincent!'

James muttered an expletive. 'Did Melanie sharpen your tongue while she was using the scissors?' he snapped angrily. 'Just who do you think you're talking to, young Domine?'

'Don't patronize me!' she was exclaiming indignantly, when she became aware that they had an audience. A woman had come to stand at the door of the lounge and was regarding them with obvious interest. It was not Yvonne Park, as Domine had half expected, but an older woman, a woman of perhaps James Mannering's own age, but beautifully made up to look years younger. She was wearing a close-fitting dress of mauve lurex-threaded jersey and her hair was the same silvery blonde as Yvonne's, but whereas Yvonne's had been curly, this woman's was straight and clung to her head like a cap. She was small and slim, with delicate features, and there were rings on every one of her slender fingers.

'What's going on, James?' she asked, in a husky voice that bore the faintest trace of an accent. 'Who is this? Your ward?'

James turned, and seemed to suppress a gesture of impatience, before he spoke. 'Oh, yes, Lucia,' he said, at last, 'this is my – ward, Domine Grainger. Domine, this is Signora Marcinello.'

Domine stepped forward, over the suitcases, and shook hands with the Italian woman rather reluctantly. This was the widow that Melanie had been talking about, the one whose husband had killed himself.

'How do you do, Signora,' she said politely. 'Did you have a good journey?'

Lucia Marcinello smiled rather languidly. 'It was as well as could be expected on your crowded English roads,' she exclaimed. Then she touched her forehead lightly with lacquered fingertips. 'James, did you get my aspirin?'

James withdrew his gaze from Domine's stubborn young face, and took his hands from his pockets. 'God, no!' he exclaimed. 'I forgot all about them. Where did you say they were?'

'In the glove compartment, darling,' murmured Lucia, running a hand across the smooth material of his suit. 'I'm sorry to be such a nuisance . . .'

'It's no bother,' replied James pleasantly, and leaving the two women together he opened the front door and disappeared down the steps. Lucia's attention returned to Domine, and taking her arm she drew her into the lounge.

'Come,' she said, 'we must get acquainted. So you are Domine! You are much different from my expectations. James told me you were little more than a child.'

Domine controlled her expression. 'Ja – I mean, my guardian, is rather old-fashioned,' she replied, with composure. 'He imagines anyone under the age of twenty-one still drinks milk out of a bottle – with a teat!' She smiled rather sardonically, and Lucia looked

123

surprised.

'Is that how you think he imagines you?' she asked.
'No, I do not believe it! But you are young, touchingly
so.'

Domine compressed her lips. 'Are you staying long,
Signora?'

Lucia Marcinello sank back in her chair and put a
weary hand to her brow. 'Oh, I do not know,' she
replied. 'But I had to get away from London. The
press, you know?' She sighed heavily. 'They will not
leave you alone. If they think you have some lurid story
to tell them, your life is not your own until it is told.'
She glanced round as James came back into the room,
and accepted the tablets he handed her, catching his
hand as well and imprisoning it in two of hers. 'But
James has been so understanding, haven't you, darling?
He offered me this place as a kind of retreat, and I
jumped at the chance. Anywhere I might go belonging
to Giulio will already have been covered by the press.
But this place is so lonely, so secure, somehow. I'm sure
no one will find me here, James.'

'Let's hope not,' he replied, a trifle shortly, and
straightened, withdrawing his hand from Lucia's as
Melanie came into the room from the kitchen pushing
a trolley on which was a jug of coffee, some sandwiches,
and a thick cream sponge. 'Thank you, Melanie,'
James nodded, taking the trolley and wheeling it across
the room for her. 'It was good of you to bother.'

Melanie shrugged. 'It was nothing,' she said
indifferently. 'You don't mind if I leave you to it now,
do you? It's late, and I have an early call.'

'Won't you join us for coffee?' protested Lucia appealingly. 'I have been such a nuisance—'

'No, thank you,' Melanie interrupted her, and gave
Domine a nod. 'Hello there,' she said. 'Did you have a

good time?'

Domine nodded, and as Melanie made for the door, she hastened after her, 'Domine!' That was James. 'Where are you going?'

Domine turned apprehensively. 'To bed,' she answered briefly.

Lucia's eyes were wide. 'Oh, surely not?'

'I – I have an early call, too,' Domine excused herself, and without waiting to see James's annoyance, she went out of the room with Melanie.

In the hall, she caught the older girl's arm, and whispered: 'When did they arrive?'

Melanie shrugged. 'Just before you did.'

'And where's Mrs. Mannering?'

Melanie half-smiled. 'She suddenly developed a severe headache and had to go to bed,' she replied, shaking her head. 'She's not going to like this at all!'

Domine nodded. 'No, I can understand that.'

Melanie shrugged again, and put her arm across Domine's shoulders. 'Come on,' she said. 'Don't look so downcast. I gather from the argument that ensued in the hall while I was making supper that James didn't exactly enthuse about your appearance.'

'Enthuse?' echoed Domine gloomily. 'He practically said I looked a mess!' She sighed. 'Oh, Melanie, why has he brought that woman here?'

Melanie frowned. 'Well, you heard what she said. I suppose that was why.'

'And do you think there's anything – I mean – do you think she's his – well – mistress?' She flushed scarlet.

Melanie chuckled as they began to climb the stairs together. 'That's a good old-fashioned word, if you like,' she commented cheerfully. 'And as to the answer – well, I should hardly think it's likely. After all, Signora Marcinello has just been widowed and James does have some sense of propriety.'

Domine wondered why she should feel such an immense sensation of relief at Melanie's words. It was disturbing to consider that her own demeanour depended wholly on the actions of the man who had constituted himself her guardian.

CHAPTER SEVEN

THE next morning Domine was up early as usual, and was helping Melanie to feed the animals when James came strolling into the stable yard. He was alone, and Domine wondered how the immaculate Signora Marcinello was this morning. Certainly, she would find all the peace she needed at Grey Witches providing she did not get involved with Mrs. Mannering.

James frowned when he saw Domine carrying two buckets of water, and said sharply: 'Just how long has this been going on?'

Domine stood down her burden and straightened. 'Just how long has what been going on?' she asked coolly. 'My helping Melanie?'

'Yes.'

She shrugged. 'Almost since I came. You knew I helped about the farm.'

James thrust his hands impatiently into his trousers pockets. 'I knew you helped, yes,' he agreed, 'but not to this extent or at this hour!' He chewed his lip, looking across at Melanie. 'Well?' he said accusingly.

Melanie heaved a sigh. 'She doesn't have to do it.'

Domine compressed her lips angrily. Once again he was trying to put her in her place. 'No, I don't,' she said now, backing up Melanie's statement. 'But I like to – and I want to! Contrary to any notions you might have had about my life previously, we were not left to laze around at the convent. There was plenty for us to do, and we did it. And what's more, we enjoyed doing it!' She hunched her shoulders. 'You don't live here, Mr. Mannering, so don't expect to come back on visits and throw your weight around so far as my activities are concerned!'

As soon as the words were out, Domine longed to withdraw them. Even Melanie was looking slightly uncomfortable, and James Mannering looked positively furious.

'Now wait a minute!' he muttered harshly, 'I do not intend to listen to that kind of impudence from you! Obviously, things have been happening in my absence, and not for the better!' He looked across at Melanie. 'What have you been telling this girl?'

Melanie shrugged awkwardly. 'Nothing, absolutely nothing.' She sniffed thoughtfully. 'If you ask me, she's just getting wise to the world in general and you in particular!'

'What's that supposed to mean?'

Now Melanie coloured. 'Oh – nothing,' she muttered. 'Look, excuse me, will you? I've got work to do!' and she turned and went into the barn.

After she had gone, Domine bent to lift her buckets again, but he prevented her, his hand on her wrist. 'Not yet,' he muttered bleakly. 'I want to talk to you.'

Domine sighed. 'Can't it wait?' she asked rudely.

'No, damn you, it can't,' he replied angrily. 'Get your horse! We're going riding!'

Domine wanted to refuse, but she didn't dare. There was something about his expression that brooked no interference in his plans, and with ill grace she saddled Rosie and rode ahead of him out of the yard.

Once on the moors however, some of her apprehension disappeared in the pure joy of being free of any constraint for a while. She sighed almost contentedly, hardly aware of the contemplative gaze of her companion.

Weatherwise, it was not a promising morning.

Ahead of them, to the south, storm clouds were rolling up, giving the moors a strange and brooding air, while the coastline was obscured by a veil of mist. The atmosphere was damp and chilling, and Domine shivered. She was just wearing a chunky sweater over an old tee-shirt of Melanie's. Once she glanced round, and saw that the house and its surrounding buildings had been swallowed up in the mist, and there was something a little unnerving about being out on the moors with a man to whom she had shown so little respect.

At last, when she was beginning to wonder whether he intended to speak to her at all, he said: 'We'll stop here. There's a shelter I found once, when I was a boy, and we can talk. At least it will be dry.'

Domine hesitated, but when he dismounted she waited only a moment before following suit. They were standing on the brink of a steep incline and James took his horse's reins and led him down the steep slope and under an overhanging bluff of rock. Frowning, Domine followed his example, and found to her surprise that beneath the bluff there was a kind of shallow cave; a rocky opening hidden by undergrowth and clumps of prickly gorse. James had already tethered his horse to one of the overhanging bushes, and Domine fastened Rosie's reins beside the hunter's, before taking a good look around. James was standing just inside the mouth of the cave, and she could see that there were no hidden caverns beyond, just a concave wall of rock.

James felt in his pocket and brought out a packet of cigarettes, extracting one and lighting it thoughtfully while his eyes watched Domine. Domine moved nervously. She felt rather like she might have done had she been summoned to Reverend Mother's study at the convent. There was about James Mannering the same kind of censure. As he drew on his cigarette, making no immediate move towards telling her why he wanted to talk to her, she said, a little recklessly:

'Couldn't we get on with this? I mean — it's not exactly cosy here, is it?' She bit her lip. 'If you're going to humiliate me, why don't you get it over with?'

His eyes darkened. 'Stop speaking to me as though I were an enemy,' he exclaimed irritatedly. 'I don't know what's got into you. When I brought you here, we could at least talk to one another.'

'Could we?' Domine kicked at a stone restlessly. 'It was you who said men and women were always antagonists, remember?'

He half-smiled. 'You're taking my words out of context. Our relationship is not that of a man and a woman!'

'Oh, no,' she flared. 'That's right! I forgot who I was talking to for a moment! I'd put my toys away in your absence. I shall have to take them out again!' She hunched her shoulders and sighed. 'Oh, why do you make me say these things?' she asked unhappily. 'I'm not a shrew, I'm not! But you won't ever treat me like an equal!'

He studied her countenance shrewdly. 'Very well, Domine, when you stop behaving like a child, I'll stop treating you like one.'

Her eyes flickered, but she said nothing, and he went on: 'I wanted to talk to you about Lucia.'

'Oh, yes?' Domine sounded disinterested. Always, after a few minutes in his presence, she felt this overwhelming sense of inadequacy. She always seemed to expect something exhilarating to happen, but nothing ever did, only this awful sense of anti-climax.

'Yes,' he said now. 'What do you think of her?'

Domine shrugged. 'I can hardly see that my opinion matters,' she said evasively.

James compressed his lips. 'Lucia is going to stay at Grey Witches. I want you two to like one another.'

Domine wrinkled her nose. 'We're not characters in one of your plays, you know,' she countered tartly. 'We can't be made to like one another just because you want it that way.'

James was controlling his temper with obvious difficulty. 'From that remark, I gather you didn't like her,' he said harshly.

Domine shrugged. 'She's very – decorative,' she commented half-contemptuously.

'And you were very rude to her last night,' he went on, quietly. 'You didn't even say good night.'

Domine coloured. 'I could see you didn't want me around,' she retorted.

James threw his cigarette stub on the ground and stood on it firmly. 'Are you trying to say something, Domine?' he asked ominously.

Domine fingered the stonework at the entrance to the cave. 'Can I ask you something?'

He shrugged. 'If you like. I won't promise to answer you.'

Domine lifted her shoulders. 'Well, you tell me, why did you bring her here?'

He ran a hand through his hair. 'Like she said, the press were hounding her.'

'And you felt sorry for her?'

'Something like that.'

'How touching!' Domine was openly contemptuous now. 'There should be headlines about you, really there should; *James Mannering, the successful playwright, rescues yet another damsel in distress. Only six weeks ago, he offered a home to the orphaned daughter of his . . .*' She halted, half mockingly, half uncertainly. 'What could we say your relationship was to

my great-uncle?' Her words were deliberately taunt-
ing, and she knew it, but some devil inside her, some
desire for revenge, made her go on.

'You little—' He bit off the word, grasping her wrist
and dragging her towards him. 'You deserve a thrash-
ing for that!'

Domine was trembling but unrepentant. 'Promises,
promises!' she murmured provocatively, and then
gasped in horror when he dragged her across to the
back of the cave where a rim of rock provided sitting
space. Pulling her down across his knees, he proceeded
to administer several hard slaps to her rear end, and
despite all her struggling, she could not escape him.

When he finally set her on her feet, she was almost
crying, her eyes filled with unshed tears. 'You – you
beast!' she stammered, trying to restore a little order to
her rumpled garments. 'Oh, how – how could you?'

He rose beside her, looking down at her solemnly.
'Don't pretend you didn't ask for it,' he muttered savagely, his eyes dark and disturbed. 'I'm sorry if I hurt
you, but you've got to realize—'

'What have I got to realize?' she exclaimed tremulously. 'That because I'm temporarily in your care, you
can do what you like with me? That you can beat me if
you want to?'

'I didn't beat you!' he snapped furiously, 'and you
know it! I merely administered a salutory punishment!'

'A salutory punishment!' she echoed. 'And would
you do the same sort of thing to Lucia Marcinello if she
dared to answer you back? Or Yvonne Park? Or
Melanie, perhaps?'

'Don't be ridiculous!' he said fiercely, raking a hand
through his hair.

'What's so ridiculous?' She moved closer to him,

looking up at him with derision in her eyes. 'Of course, I was forgetting, they're all victims to the fatal Mannering charm! What ways would a woman like Lucia Marcinello use to persuade you to understand her point of view? I realize my methods are rather inexperienced and unsophisticated, and I foolishly say what I think without guarding my tongue, but there must be ways . . .'

'I warn you, Domine,' he began.

'Warn me?' She bit back the tears burning at the back of her eyes. 'What possible punishment can you offer now? You've done everything it's in your power to do. You could confiscate my new clothes, of course, or forbid me to leave the house, but—'

'Stop it!' He almost shouted the words. 'I brought you here for one reason, to discuss Lucia's arrival and its possible effects on your position. But what happens? You deliberately turn the slight chance of communication into a kind of unholy crusade against supposed injustices! I get enough of that kind of thing from my mother, or hadn't you noticed?'

Domine sniffed unhappily. 'Well, you certainly put me straight,' she murmured chokingly. 'I didn't think even you—' Her voice broke, and she turned away, breathing swiftly, trying to quell her tears.

'Oh, Domine, for God's sake!' he groaned, half-impatiently. 'All right, all right, I'm sorry! I lost my temper, and that was unforgivable. I'm sorry.' He heaved a sigh. 'But you goaded me beyond endurance! The last couple of weeks have been hell! I've been averaging three or four hours' sleep in every twenty-four, and coming back here to confront a raging virago is not my idea of relaxation!' He shook his head. 'I'm not trying to excuse my actions, I'm just trying to explain—' He broke off, swinging her round to face him.

'Are you listening to me?'

Domine rubbed the back of her hand wearily across her eyes. 'Every word,' she answered in a small voice. 'All right, you've explained your reasons, so can we go home?'

'Domine!' His voice was taut. 'What would you have me say? I've apologized! What more can I do?'

Domine lifted her shoulders. 'Nothing, of course,' she replied, dully, assailed by an awful sense of desolation.

'Domine,' he said again, pleadingly. 'Look at me!' and when she did so: 'Have you forgiven me?'

Domine bit her lip hard. 'I'm not going to ease your conscience by saying yes,' she replied, with a return of her indignation.

His fingers suddenly gripped her forearms tightly, and he stared at her with tormented eyes. 'You certainly want your pound of flesh, don't you?' he muttered thickly. 'All right, Domine, you shall have it—' and he pulled her trembling body close against the hard length of his own. Cupping her chin with one hand, he forced her to look up at him, and she quivered beneath the gaze of those brilliant blue eyes. Then his mouth came down on hers, forcing her lips apart, searching and demanding, destroying all the frail imaginings she had cherished of what a kiss might be. His hands slid round her back, caressing her waist, pressing her closer against him so that she could feel the heat of his body warming hers to life. While his mouth caressed every inch of her face and throat he unfastened her braid, threading his fingers through it so that it fell in a silky curtain about her shoulders. When his mouth returned to hers, her lips parted involuntarily, and as he buried his face in her hair, she slid her arms around his neck, drawing him closer.

She didn't know how long she was in his arms, she only knew that it was long enough to realize that this was where she wanted to be. He had awoken something inside her which had previously lain dormant, unaware of its potential, but now she knew the need of a woman for a man, and the hunger that only complete surrender could assuage.

But even as she became aware of these desires, she felt something wet hit her arm, and then something else, and presently a steady splattering of water covered them. The discovery that it was raining now, and quite heavily, the water penetrating the overhanging shrubs, was sufficient to bring James to his senses, and he thrust Domine away from him almost violently.

'My God!' he muttered, shaking his head. 'Thank heaven for the storm! I must be going out of my mind!'

Domine stared at him shakily, aware of a look of loathing on his dark face. Turning, she stared out at the prematurely darkened sky, and the steady wall of rain that fell outside their small shelter. The mist had been lifted, but the visibility was still obscured by the rain, and she glanced down at the scarcity of protection a sweater and pants would offer. As though endeavouring to behave naturally, James said, in a taut voice:

'There's no point in both of us getting wet. I'll ride back with the horses, and bring the Rover out to collect you.'

Domine chewed at her lips. 'I don't want to stay here,' she replied, shivering. 'I'd rather take my chance in the storm.'

'But it's pouring,' he exclaimed impatiently. 'You'd

catch your death of cold. It won't take me many minutes, and you'll be quite safe here.'

'I want to come with you,' she begged pleadingly. 'Oh, James, don't start looking angry again! What was so terrible about kissing me? Didn't you want to kiss me?'

His eyes darkened momentarily. 'You must know what I wanted to do,' he muttered, rather thickly. 'But I despise the impulse!'

'Why? *Why?*' She swept back her hair from her face.

'Because you're a great many years younger than I am, and I'm your accepted guardian into the bargain!' he replied heavily. 'I can't apologize again. But if it's any consolation, I don't have much self-respect!'

'But you'll admit I'm not a child,' she exclaimed urgently.

He brushed past her, dragging the reins of the hunter from the bushes. 'No,' he muttered savagely, 'you're not a child!' He glanced back at her half angrily. 'And if it pleases you, you have the power to infuriate me into actions I would otherwise believe myself incapable of.' He looked up at the lowering sky. 'But it won't happen again. I promise you that.'

Domine's heart sank and out of the bitterness in her soul she taunted him: 'How can you be sure?'

He mounted the hunter expertly, and looked down at her. 'Because I intend to place a considerable distance between us,' he replied harshly. 'And the sooner the better!'

Domine bent her head. 'You think you can plan your life so emotionlessly,' she said unsteadily. She looked up. 'Don't emotions count for anything with you?'

He shrugged. 'Not a lot. What kind of emotions were

you thinking of?'

'How about – love?' she murmured quietly.

'Love?' There was a cruel glint to his eyes. 'What is love? I doubt if you know, and I admit I don't. That's a luxury that's always been denied me.'

'Your mother loves you!' exclaimed Domine.

'Does she? Or does she love the power that I unwittingly placed into her hands?' He gave a scornful laugh. 'And if you imagine the sexual urgency which we just shared has anything to do with that sweet emotion, then kill the thought. I admit – I wanted you, Domine. For my sins, I can't deny it. But with you – or anyone else – the result would have been just as satisfying!' and with that, he wheeled his horse and rode away.

Domine stared after him, mounting the bluff and watching him press the hunter into a gallop. She felt the hot tears rolling unheeded down her cheeks, mingling with the rain, the only difference being the salty tang on her lips. Oh, how could he, how could he? she thought agonizingly. Were all men like him? Had they all this appetite that any woman could satisfy?

Feeling sick with unhappiness, she slid back down the slope and untethered Rosie. At least he had not taken her horse, and if his intention was to return for her, then he was wasting his time. She had no intention of remaining here to wait for him and then have to endure the torture of riding home with him in the Land-Rover. She didn't much care just then whether she got back to Grey Witches or not. Just so long as she didn't have to spend any time alone in his presence until she had succeeded in gathering her pitiful store of defences about her.

As luck would have it, Melanie saw her enter the

stable yard, and Domine supposed she would inform her cousin that his ward had arrived back safely. Avoiding any conversation with the older girl, Domine just called:

'Can I leave Rosie to one of the men? I'm soaked to the skin!' and when Melanie nodded and began to walk towards her, Domine disappeared hastily into the house. She ran across the hall, and was mounting the stairs when she encountered Mrs. Mannering on her way down.

'Domine!' she exclaimed, halting her with a fastidious hand. 'Whatever have you been doing to yourself? You're soaked! And your hair – what's happened to your braid?'

Domine bent her head, avoiding Mrs. Mannering's eyes. 'I – I caught it on the – the—' she sought about wildly for an answer, and finally came up with: '—on the branch of a tree. I – I was hurrying home in the storm, and I suppose I was clumsy.'

It wasn't much of an explanation and Mrs. Mannering frowned rather suspiciously. 'You haven't been meeting Vincent out on the moors, have you?' she queried.

Domine heaved a sigh. 'No – no, of course not.'

'But you were late home last evening, weren't you?'

'Yes. I'm sorry. I'll make sure I'm not so late again.'

Mrs. Mannering nodded. 'Good. Did you – meet our new guest?'

'Signora Marcinello? Yes, I did.'

'What did you think of her?' Mrs. Mannering's frown deepened. 'James seems to imagine he can bring all his lame ducks here.'

Domine could hardly imagine that 'lame duck' was a reasonable description of someone as beautiful as

Lucia Marcinello, but she presumed it was a kind of inverted dig at herself. However, she said rather tentatively: 'Signora Marcinello seems to need peace and quiet. At least, that's what she said.'

'Did she now? Well, she's brought sufficient baggage to equip her for an indefinite stay. So long as she realizes this is not an hotel, and I'm not going to spend my time running about after *her*! I have enough to do as it is. I think it was most unreasonable of James to foist his—'

Domine interrupted her. 'Look,' she said pleasantly, 'can we leave this conversation until later? I'm frozen and I'm dripping water all over the stairs . . .'

Mrs. Mannering shrugged her shoulders with ill grace. 'Oh, very well,' she snapped, 'go about your business! Don't let me hinder you! It's obvious that no one gives a damn for my feelings. And even Melanie seem less than interested in James's new girl-friend!'

'Signora Marcinello has just been widowed,' Domine pointed out, shivering a little.

'Do you think that matters to a woman like her!' Mrs. Mannering was contemptuous. 'Not at all! I've no doubt they imagine they can indulge themselves in an illicit affair here, miles away from annoying publicists and the like! Well, they're mistaken! I won't have it, do you hear? I won't have it. Not in my house!'

Domine could have pointed out that this was not *her* house, it was James's, but she hadn't the energy to argue with her. Instead she merely nodded sympathetically, and excusing herself ran the rest of the way to her room.

Once there, she stripped off all her garments, for she was indeed soaked to the skin and even her bra and panties were clinging wetly to her. She ran herself a steaming bath and was about to get into it when Lucy called that breakfast was ready. Ignoring the summons, Domine added some perfumed salts to the water and climbed into its warming depths with relief. The heat of the water was balm to her chilled flesh, and she slid down so that it could cover her shoulders completely.

She lay there supine for almost half an hour, refusing to think of anything but the numbing temperature of the water. The haze of steam surrounded her, and she could have closed her eyes and banished all unwelcome thoughts in oblivion. But instead, after warming herself all through, she sat up and began to soap her body. As her misty brain began to re-assert itself, she was forced to admit thoughts of James Mannering, and the anxieties that this morning's events aroused in her. She could not dismiss what had happened as he appeared to have done. For her it had closed one chapter in her life, and opened another, and no matter how many men she might know in the future no one else would awaken her as James's touch had done. There had been a kind of suppressed violence in his lovemaking that had struck an answering chord inside her, and his expertise had taken her to the brink of ecstasy. A warm heat ran over her body as she recalled his caressing touch, and then it was followed by the chilling realization that she was not the first woman who had felt like this after being with him. Or the last! Her tortured brain mocked her.

With jerky movements she climbed out of the bath, wrapping herself in the bath towel and drying her body thoroughly. As she did so, waves of heat and cold ran over her persistently, and she realized that it wasn't just thoughts of James that were causing these physical sensations. She felt chilled to the bone, and even though she wrapped herself up warmly in a thick skirt and a couple of sweaters she still felt cold.

When she could no longer delay the inevitable, she descended the stairs and came upon Melanie in the hall. She, too, was wet, but a mackintosh prevented her from getting soaked through.

'Is it still raining?' asked Domine, sniffing, and taking out a handkerchief to wipe her nose.

Melanie frowned. 'Yes, it's still raining,' she agreed. 'What's up, Domine? You look terrible! What did James say to you out there on the moors?'

Domine shook her head. The last thing she wanted was a cosy confidential talk with Melanie. 'Nothing,' she denied, flushing. 'Ooh, I'm frozen. I hope there's a good fire in the lounge.' Although the house was centrally heated, Henry Farriday had always kept a fire in the main room.

Melanie shrugged her shoulders. 'Okay, keep it to yourself,' she said resignedly. 'I'm going for a wash. There's nothing much to do outside in this weather. You missed breakfast. Weren't you hungry?'

'I was in the bath,' explained Domine, shivering 'Where – where is everybody?'

'Aunt Geraldine is in the kitchen, and Signora Marcinello asked for a breakfast tray in her room. James took it up.'

'I – I see.' Domine managed a slight smile at the older girl before leaving her to enter the lounge. She was glad the room was empty, for she dragged her chair up to the fire, and warmed her hands at the flames. Obviously she had caught a chill, but compared to her emotional state it was a very paltry thing.

Presently Mrs. Mannering came in and joined her. 'Ah, there you are, Domine,' she exclaimed. 'Did you not want any breakfast?'

Domine shook her head. 'I was in the bath,' she explained again.

'Never mind.' Mrs. Mannering settled herself on the couch. 'Lucy is bringing me some coffee in a few minutes. You can share that.'

'Thank you,' Domine smiled, and resumed her contemplation of the flames.

'Have you heard? Signora Marcinello wanted a tray in her room,' remarked Mrs. Mannering, picking up the morning paper and scanning its headlines casually. 'I refused to have anything to do with it, of course. James has taken it up to her.'

Domine bit her lip. 'Yes, so Melanie told me.'

Mrs. Mannering nodded. 'Disgraceful, isn't it? I mean – what will the servants think?' She shrugged her narrow shoulders. 'You look as though you've caught a chill. Whatever possessed you to go riding on the moors in this awful weather?'

'It wasn't raining when we left,' pointed out Domine quietly.

'We?' Mrs. Mannering pounced on the word. 'Who is "we"?'

Domine could have bitten off her tongue. 'Er – Mr. Mannering,' she murmured uncomfortably.

'James?' Mrs. Mannering frowned. 'He was with you?'

'Yes.'

'I see.' Mrs. Mannering folded the newspaper thoughtfully. 'Did you have a row?'

Domine moved awkwardly. 'Why do you ask that?'

'Because he was like a bear with a sore head at breakfast,' replied Mrs. Mannering shortly, 'and it wasn't anything to do with me. What did you row about?'

'Did I say we did?'

'No, but it's obvious.' Mrs. Mannering grimaced. 'I suppose it was to do with that Marcinello woman.'

'No!' Domine was adamant.

'Then what?'

'Oh, it was nothing,' exclaimed Domine uncomfortably. 'I – I'd rather not discuss it, if you don't mind.'

Mrs. Mannering sighed exaggeratedly. 'Oh, I don't know why I bother even being polite!' she cried impatiently. 'Everyone seems to lead a life all their own. Have you noticed that? We're supposed to be a family, but are we? I mean – James has no time for me, and Melanie constantly infuriates me! You'd think, when I've been good enough to offer her a home, she'd feel a sense of gratitude towards me, but no!' She shook her head. 'No one cares about me at all.'

'That's not true,' remarked a voice behind them, and Domine felt her limbs turn to water as James came into the room. 'Why do you persistently behave like some tragedian heroine, Mother?' he exclaimed sardonically. 'You know perfectly well that everyone jumps to do your bidding.'

'I haven't noticed,' remarked Mrs. Mannering shortly. 'Have you given Signora Marcinello her breakfast? It's taken you long enough.'

James ignored his mother's sarcasm, and said: 'Why are you huddling over the fire, Domine? Have you caught a chill?'

Domine refused to meet his gaze. 'I've just had a bath,' she replied quietly. 'Naturally, I felt the cold after I came out.'

He came over to the fire, and stood with his back to it, looking down at her thoughtfully. Domine was conscious of the lean strength of his legs only inches from her fingers, and twisted her hands together to prevent a compulsive urge to touch him.

'You should have remained sheltering until I returned,' he said harshly. 'Do you know I wasted the time going back for you?'

Domine's head jerked up. 'You didn't really expect me to wait there like some trapped rabbit?' she flared. 'I wanted to get back.'

Mrs. Mannering's eyes widened speculatively. 'What's all this about?' she queried with interest. 'Domine?'

Domine bent her head again, and James said, pleasantly: 'It's nothing of any importance, Mother.' He took out his cigarettes and offering them to his mother he went on: 'By the way, I shall be leaving again in the morning.'

Domine forced herself not to look up, but Mrs. Mannering sounded infuriated. 'What do you mean? You're going and leaving that woman here?'

'Signora Marcinello will stay for some weeks, yes,' he agreed, nodding.

'But I don't want her here!' protested Mrs. Mannering impatiently. 'You can't expect us to entertain your women now, James!'

James's face darkened. 'Don't be coarse, Mother,' he snapped coldly. 'This is my house, and it's my money that's maintaining it. If I choose to bring a guest here, I expect my mother to show her a little honest decency! Contrary to your speculations, Lucia means absolutely nothing to me! Her husband was an acquaintance, that's all.'

Mrs. Mannering considered this. 'And how long are you going to be away?' She frowned. 'Are you going to London?'

'No, actually I'm not. I'm going to Rome,' he replied briefly.

'Rome?' echoed Mrs. Mannering. 'What for?'

James sighed impatiently. 'If you insist on knowing, then I'll tell you that I'm going to sort out Lucia's affairs for her. Giulio left everything in quite a state. Someone has to do it, and she has no one else. At least, no one she can trust.'

Domine listened with a sinking heart. He was certainly doing as he had said, and putting plenty of miles between them. Was that why he was leaving so abruptly?

'I see,' said Mrs. Mannering now. 'Oh, well, I suppose if you insist she stays, she stays. But I do think it's very inconsiderate of you. Heavens, it'll be Christmas in four weeks. Have you thought of that?'

'Of course I have,' he replied bleakly. 'Is it so inconceivable that we should have a guest for the festive season?'

'You'll be back then?'

'Of course.' He glanced at Domine. 'After all, it wouldn't be fair to Domine to subject her to a Christmas alone with three women, all of whom regard each other as antagonists.'

Domine did not respond as he had expected she might. Instead, she shrank further into her corner. He didn't care what kind of Christmas she spent. If he came back to Grey Witches it would not be for her sake, but he could hardly appraise his mother of such a damning situation.

'Oh, well,' Mrs. Mannering sighed, 'I suppose nothing I can say will change things. Domine, fetch my glasses, would you, dear? They're on the table in the hall.'

'Of course.' Domine got to her feet, and hastened out of the room, glad of the chance to escape from James Mannering's cold eyes, but to her surprise he followed her, and when she would have returned to the lounge, he prevented her, his fingers on her wrist.

'A moment,' he murmured softly, so that his mother should not hear. 'Domine, I want you to put what happened this morning right out of your mind, do you understand me? I wish to God it had never happened, but it did, and I need your assurance that you'll forget all about it!' His eyes surveyed her thoroughly, and she felt a choking sensation in her throat.

'It's forgotten,' she whispered coldly. 'Now let me go!'

'Domine,' he muttered fiercely, 'don't make this any harder for me than it is. I want you to know I don't make a habit of that kind of thing!'

'Don't you?' she exclaimed softly, her eyes unnaturally bright. 'You're amazingly expert for an amateur—'

'Domine!' He gritted his teeth, and then she was free and Melanie was running down the stairs to join them.

'Well, well,' she remarked mockingly. 'What's going on? Domine, you look positively feverish! You must have caught a chill.'

'I – I think I did,' murmured Domine uncomfortably. 'Melanie, will you give your aunt these glasses. She asked me to get them. I – I think I'll go and take some aspirin.'

Melanie nodded sympathetically. 'Yes, love, you do that,' she smiled. 'Are you coming in, James?'

James looked at Domine's retreating back as she ran up the stairs, and then turned to his cousin. 'Oh, yes, I guess so,' he muttered bleakly, and followed her into the lounge.

In her bedroom, Domine flung herself face down on the bed. She had never felt so utterly miserable in all her life. Her future seemed to stretch away ahead of her, bare and uninteresting, and the knowledge that James was leaving again in the morning was tearing her apart.

CHAPTER EIGHT

By the evening of that day Domine's cold had developed into quite a fever, but she dosed herself well and crept into bed without telling anyone. She had succeeded in avoiding everybody for the whole day, using her cold as an excuse and remaining in her room. It was a cowardly action, she realized, but she had no strength to fight her traitorous emotions right now.

In the morning she felt too weak to crawl out of bed, and there was an awful tightness in her chest. Lily came to see how she was and expressed concern at her pale cheeks and breathlessness.

'You need a doctor, miss,' she exclaimed anxiously. 'I'll tell Mrs. Mannering. She'll send for Doctor Rivers.'

'No.' Domine coughed a little. 'I'm all right. If I stay in bed today, I'll be fine tomorrow.'

Lily shook her head. 'You could be much worse tomorrow,' she said, frowning. 'Let me tell Mrs. Mannering. I can't leave you like this.'

Domine shook her head weakly. 'No, please!' she begged. 'Let – let Mr. Mannering get away. I – I don't want him to stay here because of me ...' She heaved a sigh. 'Tell them I still have my cold, and I'm staying in my room. No one need suspect ...'

Lily tucked the covers about her and put her cool hand to Domine's hot forehead. 'You must be running a temperature sky-high!' she protested.

Domine closed her eyes for a moment. 'Look, Lily, just let Mr. Mannering get away. Then – then you can tell Mrs. Mannering – all right?'

Lily looked doubtful. 'Don't you think Mr. James ought to know, too? After all, you are his ward.'

'What ought I to know, Lily?' queried a lazy voice from the doorway, and both women started guiltily, Domine's fingers clenching the silk coverlet convulsively. James walked slowly into the room, coming to the bed and looking down at Domine's flushed cheeks. 'So?' he said quietly, 'I was right. You do have a chill.'

Domine moved restlessly under his gaze. 'It's nothing,' she protested unhappily, aware of the steely quality of his eyes.

Lily wrung her hands together. 'I'm so glad you've come, sir,' she exclaimed. 'Miss Grainger ought to have a doctor, really she should. I think she's running a temperature.'

'I think so, too, Lily,' he remarked, in agreement. 'Can you call Dr. Rivers' house? Do you know the number?'

'Yes, sir.'

'Then go ahead. Whatever Miss Grainger says, she does require medical attention.'

'Yes, sir. Thank you, sir,' Lily nodded, and darted from the room while James continued to study Domine thoughtfully.

'Why didn't you want me to know?' he asked harshly.

Domine compressed her lips. 'I knew you were leaving this morning. I didn't want to – to – worry you,' she murmured miserably.

'You knew I wouldn't go leaving you in this state,' he muttered angrily. 'What do you take me for? This is all my fault, and you know it!'

Domine turned on her side away from him. 'It's my

149

own fault,' she replied resignedly. 'If I hadn't insisted on returning on my own yesterday, I wouldn't have caught the cold.'

'Agreed. But as it was at my insistence you were out on the moors at all, I feel entirely responsible.' He walked away from the bed to stand at the window, looking out at the day. A wind howled round the old eaves of the building, and the rain had given way to a dampness in the air.

Domine sighed, and rolled on to her back. There was a pain in her chest, and she wished he would go so that she could give way to a spasm of coughing that was rising inside her. She didn't want him here, witnessing her weakness.

Swallowing hard, she said: 'I wish you would go.' She brushed back her hair with a careless hand. 'You've done your duty – you've called the doctor – now leave me alone!'

James turned to stare at her coldly. 'Don't give me orders, Domine,' he snapped. He walked away from the window, and stood at the foot of the bed. 'But I will go – and I'll see you later, after Doctor Rivers has been.'

Domine nodded, and deliberately closed her eyes so that he should think she wanted to rest. With an impatient exclamation he walked to the door, and presently she heard it slam behind him. It had not been a hard slam, just a kind of controlled closing of the door that somehow went awry.

As soon as the door closed, Domine heaved a sigh of relief, and rolling weakly out of the bed she padded across to the dressing table. She stared with displeasure at the unhealthy flush high on her cheekbones in a face that was otherwise devoid of colour. She looked terrible, and hunched her shoulders wearily. She hadn't wanted him to see her like this, so weak and unattractive. Why couldn't she have waited one more day before developing these symptoms? It seemed as though he was always to see her in an unattractive light. She sighed again. Not that it mattered, really. She couldn't begin to compete with a woman like Lucia Marcinello, or Yvonne Park either, for that matter. Another fit of coughing sent her stumbling back to her bed to slide beneath the covers tiredly, tucking the covers closely round her chin. Maybe if Dr. Rivers thought her condition was not very serious James would leave today as he had planned.

But in fact it was two weeks before James actually left. Dr. Rivers pronounced that Domine had bronchitis, and must stay in bed. He also told her in no uncertain terms that she was very lucky it had not deteriorated into pneumonia, considering the careless attitude she appeared to adopt towards her health.

For several days Domine was too exhausted by the congestion in her chest to care what went on around her and cared little for anybody's company. Mrs. Mannering came daily to inquire after her progress, but it was a perfunctory courtesy which she accomplished in double quick time, and Domine suspected that had James gone away as he had intended her condition would have been a matter for dispute. She had the feeling that Mrs. Mannering considered her rather inconsiderate, falling ill like this just when she had an unexpected, and unwanted, guest and a lot of extra work to see to. But as James was there, she confined herself to sarcastic remarks that mostly Domine ignored.

James himself was a frequent visitor, but Domine dreaded his coming. It wasn't that he was unkind to her, indeed his attitude towards her was remarkably gentle, but somehow by its very content, their relationship was false. Maybe, she speculated cynically, he was endeavouring to resume their earlier impersonal association before their involvement had become such an aggressive thing. Even so, despite her misgivings, Domine found this new side of James's character interested her, and certainly she learned a lot about him during these periods. He told her of the problems he faced with his writing, and the different aspects of writing for television and the theatre. Domine asked intelligent questions and presently he began to bring manuscripts for her to read, asking her opinion, listening to her tentative suggestions. While they had never been so unrestrained in one another's company in one sense, in another the tension increased, ready to be thrust disturbingly to the surface by the merest suggestion of intimacy.

Melanie was the one person Domine could relax completely with, and she came after dinner every evening with a fund of amusing anecdotes about the day's events. Mrs. Mannering and the fiery Signora Marcinello seemed to spend their lives conducting a kind of armed truce from which border flare-ups continually erupted, and James avoided confrontations between them. Melanie herself insisted she missed Domine's help, and urged her to recover quickly so that she could enjoy the preparations for the Christmas season which would soon be starting. She also kept Domine in touch with Vincent. Although that young man had come to the house, inquiring about Domine, he had not been admitted, and Melanie couldn't decide on whose intructions his dismissal had been executed. In any event, he persistently sent Domine gifts of fruit and magazines which Melanie brought up to her. Once he sent an enormous bouquet of chrysanthemums, their curly heads burgeoning in a variety of colours.

Later in the day when James made his appearance, he looked with surprise on their perfection and said, rather tautly: 'Where did these come from?'

'Melanie brought them up,' explained Domine cautiously. 'Vincent sent them for me. Aren't they magnificent?'

'Yes, magnificent,' he echoed, in a rather strange tone, then took himself off rather abruptly, leaving Domine feeling rather distrait. Despite her nervousness with him, she couldn't deny she enjoyed his visits these days and the opportunities given her for expressing herself.

As her cough improved, so too did Domine's appearance, the lazy days of good food and little exercise putting flesh on her thin limbs. She had taken to combing her hair out of its braid in the mornings and securing it with a wide Alice band which Melanie gave her, and the style suited her youthful appearance and banished the schoolroom air she had felt her plait engendered. When Dr. Rivers said she could get up for a while, she seated herself at the window in her room, still in her pyjamas, and wrapped in a warm rug from the bed until Melanie lent her a dressing gown of quilted cotton that although looking slightly washed out was nevertheless warmer and more convenient than the rug.

However, one afternoon Lucia Marcinello paid her an unexpected visit, bringing with her a cardboard box which she placed on Domine's lap.

'There,' she said, in her attractive voice. 'A present! And how are you today?'

Domine didn't know what to say, but she smiled and said she felt much better before opening the box.

Inside, wrapped in tissue paper, was a pure silk dressing gown in a delicious shade of apricot. Its clear bright colour was a perfect foil for Domine's chestnut hair and olive skin, and she looked up at the older woman in surprise.

'Oh, but I couldn't accept this from you . . .' she began, awkwardly. 'It's very kind of you, but it's obviously new, and I couldn't—'

'What nonsense is this!' exclaimed the Signora loudly. 'You would reject my gift! It is not good enough for you perhaps?'

Domine sighed. 'Of course that isn't so. It's beautiful – beautiful . . .' Her voice was a trifle wistful. 'But – well, I couldn't take it.'

'Then I shall be most offended!' cried Lucia Marcinello, rather angrily. 'Come, surely you can see, it is not a colour that would suit me. It was an – unwanted gift. Take it, I want you to have it.'

Domine hesitated, and then smiled. 'Oh, very well, then, thank you. But I really feel sure you shouldn't have given it to me.'

Lucia Marcinello waved an expressive arm, and seated herself in the chair opposite Domine in the window, looking out with interest. Then she shivered, folding her hands in her lap. 'These moors, they are so – so . . .' She gestured again. 'The loneliness is a little frightening, is it not? Me, I have been used to cities all my life, big cities like Rome, or Paris, or London.' She frowned. 'But this is not so with you, is it? James tells me you have been educated at a convent, is this so?'

Domine nodded. 'Yes. When my parents were killed my great-uncle sort of – adopted me. He paid for my schooling.'

'I see. This is James's father, of course.' At Domine's astounded expression, she smiled understandingly. 'Ah, you thought I did not know of the relationship.' She shrugged. 'This kind of situation is not new, nor very original. The extraordinary part is wondering where James got his talent from.' She rolled her eyes heavenward. 'Certainly not from the redoubtable Mrs. Mannering!' She raised both her hands. 'That woman, she is such a trial to her son!'

'I think she's very ambitious for James,' remarked Domine quietly, not wanting to discuss James's mother with this woman.

Lucia lifted her shoulders. 'This is ambition?' She shook her head. 'I think not. She is possessive. She expects James to adhere to her rules and makes no concessions. She should be aware by this time that James is not a man to be manipulated by a woman – any woman!'

Domine sighed and changed the subject. 'How are you settling down here, Signora Marcinello?' she queried politely.

Lucia shrugged her slim shoulders. In a sleek shift of lemon jersey she looked very cool and very attractive, and Domine wondered curiously what her husband had been like when he was alive. Certainly life with a woman like her would not be dull. There was an enveloping interest in her eyes when she spoke of James Mannering, and Domine thought she was the kind of woman to prefer the company of men to that of women at any time. Her enforced sojourn here at Grey Witches must tax her patience, particularly in the company of someone so infuriatingly arrogant as Geraldine Mannering. However, she said now:

'The house is an ugly old place, and the heating is antiquated, though adequate, I must admit.' She wrinkled her nose. 'But when one gets used to the isolation, one can appreciate the solitude – the peace of it all.' She sighed. 'Unfortunately, Mrs. Mannering seems bent on turning me out as soon as she is able, and I may not get the chance to settle down, as you put it.' She shrugged. 'It is Giulio, of course. His death was a terrible shock, not only to me, but to his bankers!' She shuddered. 'Mrs. Mannering is a snob!' She held up a hand as Domine would have protested: 'Don't bother to deny it, my dear, it is obvious, and while I may be socially acceptable in some ways, the scandal, and my lack of capital – er – what is that word? – they black-wash me!'

'Blackball,' Domine corrected her with a faint smile.

'Ah, yes, blackball! Yes, my circumstances are not suitable for Mrs. Mannering.' She shrugged. 'But that is unimportant. What plans have you for your future?'

Domine lay back in her chair a little wearily. 'Very few,' she confessed reluctantly.

Lucia raised her pencilled eyebrows. 'Perhaps James will find you a job in television – or the theatre,' she suggested. 'It is a very exciting world. I know. I was once a struggling actress myself. Fortunately, Giulio came along and took a fancy to me, and plucked me away from the degradation of it all!' She chuckled. 'I am joking, of course. But it can be tough – if you are not tough also.' She studied Domine appraisingly. 'You're a very attractive girl. You have good bone structure. You are not, as they say, pretty, but you are attractive. With make-up and clothes, and a little cul-tivation of your carriage, you might make a model! Does that appeal to you?'

Domine shook her head, half amused. 'You can't be serious!'

'Oh, but I am. In fact, I think that is what I may

do.' She cupped her chin on one hand thoughtfully. 'I could open a model agency. Nowadays they are always wanting models for something. All these advertisements, you know. What opportunities! ' She smiled. 'You could be my very first client.'

Domine continued to shake her head. 'Oh, I don't think so,' she protested shyly. 'But thank you for the compliment.'

Lucia shrugged. 'Maybe not, after all. I have the feeling that your guardian might not approve. Maybe he will have some plans for you. Hmm?'

'I've no idea.' Domine tried to sound casual. Then she leaned forward in her chair, and said: 'Tell me, Signora, has – has – my guardian discussed me – with you?'

Lucia Marcinello made a moue with her lips. 'From time to time,' she murmured, frowning. 'Why?'

Domine compressed her lips. It was difficult to know how to phrase it. 'Did he – I mean – am I – well—' She sighed uncomfortably, and stopped speaking.

Lucia's fingers gripped the carved arms of her chair. Smoothing the old wood, she said: 'You would like to know how James regards you, is that it?'

Domine flushed. 'Well, I was rather thrust upon him.'

Lucia nodded. 'Perhaps. Although he could have continued to pay your school fees and left you at the convent until you were eighteen, could he not?'

'I suppose so.' Domine saw the logic of that.

'Then I would think his main objective was to give you a home, a real background, if you like, not just some cold institution, little better than the orphanage you were taken from.'

'You know about that?'

'Oh, yes. As I have said, we have discussed your presence here. Let me be honest, Domine, James and I have known one another for several years. Not intimately, you understand, he was a friend of Giulio's, but to the extent of allowing confidences with one another. I think James felt sorry for you, I think he felt his father had given you a raw deal. After all, Mr. Farriday could have brought you here before this had he not been so absorbed with keeping up appearances. After all, what would you have thought of him if it had been revealed that his housekeeper was a woman he had seduced many years ago, and that James was his natural son?'

Domine pressed her hands to her cheeks. 'I don't know.'

'Exactly. You would have nurtured doubts about him, and about the reasons for his generosity, and Henry Farriday does not seem the kind of man to have wanted that. After all, he had lived an uneasy existence at best for many years. Only with you could he justify himself.'

Domine shivered. 'I suppose so,' she murmured.

'As to your future,' Lucia shrugged, 'I have the feeling that James will insist on taking quite an active part in that. With or without his condolence, you have become part of his family and I cannot quite see him dismissing his responsibilities at the end of these six months, can you?'

Domine looked up. 'Surely that's for me to decide, too?' she frowned. 'Legally, I will be independent of him then.'

'Legalities! Poof! What are legalities?' cried Lucia contemptuously. 'They are for lawyers, not for human beings with human feelings.' She leaned forward to touch Domine's hand. 'Do not be so aggressive where

James is concerned. You might have been in quite a spot with another man, a less – shall we say – scrupulous man!'

Domine got up from her chair, unable to discuss her inmost feelings with anyone, and Lucia seemed to understand that their conversation was at an end, for she rose too and said: 'So! I will go. Perhaps if I offer to help Mrs. Mannering with the household accounts she will consider I am a little less of a nuisance!' She smiled. 'Put on your dressing gown, Domine, and comb your hair. Remember always – a woman owes it to herself to be beautiful! And you are so young! That is the best thing of all.' There was a sadness in her voice before she went out of the room, leaving Domine alone.

After she had gone, Domine studied the silk gown with pleasure. It was beautiful, and it had been kind of Lucia to think of it. Very kind. And in fact she wasn't so bad after all. If James did intend to marry her, then very likely she would make him happy. Domine buried her face in the softness of the garment. This was not the time to consider James marrying. She was much too weak to contemplate such a disastrous circumstance.

When she recovered from her momentary desolation, she did as Lucia suggested and took off the cotton gown and replaced it with the apricot silk. It felt so rich, so smooth, so expensive. Taking the brush, she swept her hair back in rhythmic strokes and replaced the Alice band. What a difference it made, she thought in astonishment. The silk clung to the curves of her body lovingly, outlining the youthful slenderness of her figure, while the tie belt drew attention to the narrowness of her waist. She remembered what Lucia had said about being beautiful, and smiled. She would never be that, but perhaps she was a little more attractive than before.

Later in the day James came to see her, and although he studied her appearance very thoroughly he said nothing, neither complimenting her nor deriding her. Domine felt a rising sense of frustration at his lack of perception, and when he drew a chair up to hers and produced a scene he was having difficulty with in his new play, she felt like taking the manuscript and scattering it like confetti. But instead, she controlled her disappointment, and listened to him outlining his problems. The play was to be one of a series of six plays being produced by a major television company under a general heading of *The Profligates*. It was to be a controversial series dealing with profligacy in all its forms, from depravity to the inciting of riots. The play James was working on involved the dissolute, gambler son of hard-working parents, and the effects his conduct had on the lives of the rest of his family. It was a rather sad play, a moving portrayal of ordinary people caught up in a maelstrom of guilt and self-castigation. It was not a comfortable play, and Domine, involved in its inception, began to appreciate the brilliant talent that had made James Mannering's work so sought after. His dialogue was sharp and decisive; his characters possessed human strength as well as human failings, and his situations were a natural progression of events and not the contrived machinations of a mechanical brain. No one was all bad, just as no one was all good, and because of this the play became real – alive – identifiable.

In spite of her antipathy, Domine became interested as she always did when he talked like this to her, and it wasn't until later, when they had finished their discussion about the scene, that Domine felt a resurgence of indignation at his lack of sensitivity so far as her gown was concerned. So it was when he glanced at his watch and saw that it was already after nine-thirty and he rose to go that she said, rather petulantly:

'I can't understand why you're still here anyway. I thought you were going to Rome, to deal with Signora Marcinello's affairs.'

James put the manuscript back inside the folder he had brought it in, and then straightened, regarding her seriously. 'You are perhaps tired of our discussions?' he queried quietly.

Domine remained in her chair, refusing to look at him. Smoothing the ovals of her fingernails, shrugging, she said: 'Talking to me must be poor sport after all your intellectual friends in London.'

'You didn't answer my question,' he said,

'You didn't answer mine,' she parried swiftly.

'You want me to leave, is that it? My presence here is annoying to you?'

Domine sighed. 'Of course not. It's your house.'

James bit back an impatient expletive. 'What is the matter with you this evening?' he said, controlling his annoyance. 'I sensed from the moment I came into the room that all was not well with you. Are you feeling unwell, is that it?'

'I feel fine.' Domine compressed her lips. 'There's nothing wrong with me.'

James put down his folder and stood, hands on hips regarding her. 'Then what is it?' His eyes narrowed. 'Lucia came to see you today, did she not? What has she been saying to you?'

Domine glanced up at him. 'She was very kind,' she said expressionlessly. 'She stayed for quite a while. She brought me a present.'

James's eyes flickered. 'I know. That gown.'

Domine got indignantly to her feet. 'You knew? And

yet you still didn't say anything?'

'What would you have me say?' he inquired. 'Surely you don't need me to tell you it suits you admirably.'

Domine bent her head. 'It suits me admirably,' she echoed, almost inaudibly. 'How nice!' There was sarcasm in her tone.

She was unprepared however for the look of anguish that she surprised on his face when she looked up, and a frown darkened her brow. He seemed to be involved in some inner torment of his own, and she wondered whether he was imagining Lucia in the gown. Certainly, the Italian woman would look infinitely more alluring than she, Domine, ever could.

'Don't be bitter, Domine,' he said now, as though the words were torn from him. 'You know as well I do that our relationship is still a very fragile thing. Gradually I hope we are becoming more natural with one another again. But this antagonism, this aggressiveness, can only cause more problems. Surely you can see that?' He sighed heavily. 'Don't you think it weighs heavily on my conscience what I've done? Don't you think I'm trying to make you see me in a different light, – as I really am? Not as an animal responding blindly to the needs of the body.' His voice was harsh.

'Is that how you see it?' she demanded, hurt by his cold rejection of any kind of tenderness.

'What other way is there to see it?' he asked violently. 'But torturing myself with guilt gets us nowhere! Only by endeavouring to show you that I am not necessarily uncivilized or cruel can I attempt to redeem myself in my own eyes, let alone yours.'

Domine stared at him tremulously. 'So your time spent with me is a kind of reparation for your sins, is that it?' she cried vehemently. 'Can't you feel that what happened between us is still there, trembling below the surface of the constraint you've placed upon yourself?'

James took a deep breath, and raked a hand through his hair. 'What are you trying to do to me, Domine?' he muttered savagely. 'You've no idea of my feelings!'

'Feelings? *Feelings?*' Domine gave a mirthless laugh. 'You have no feelings. You told me that, remember? Why should I consider your feelings?'

James took a step towards her, and for a heart-shaking moment she thought he intended to strike her. Then he halted, and said: 'Oh, yes, Domine, I have feelings! But not the flaccid kind of feelings you imagine you feel! Do you think that spending time here with you alone is not a penance in itself? Talking to you, looking at you, almost touching you!' His voice was hoarse. 'I'm only flesh and blood, Domine, and as I once said, you have the capacity to disturb my mental processes without any volition on my part!' His eyes burned into hers. 'That should please you! After all, it's what you've been wanting to hear, isn't it? Does it give you a feeling of power? Does it satisfy whatever it is inside you that persistently craves a vicarious thrill?'

Domine shrank back from the suppressed violence in his tone. 'How can you say that!' she gasped in horror.

'Why not? It's the truth! You know I'm too old for you, that your emotions are simply the awakening appetites of an adolescent for male adulation!'

'That's not true!' she cried.

'Then what is the truth?' he asked contemptuously. 'I warn you, a man can only be driven so far!'

Domine twisted her hands agitatedly. 'You're just using me in an attempt to pacify your own conscience!' she said stormily, unable to quell the surge of indignation that enveloped her. 'You persistently use my age

163

as a weapon against me! Why? *Why?* Are you afraid to acknowledge that I'm a woman? Would it be so terrible? Do you fear some retribution from such a liability?'

'For God's sake, Domine, stop tormenting me!' he swore fiercely. 'Just let it go! I'll keep out of your way in future. Obviously, I was mistaken in imagining I could salvage something from the mess I created!' He bent and lifted his folder of manuscript, and as he did so a sheet of paper came loose and fluttered to the floor. Simultaneously, they both stooped to pick it up, Domine going down on her haunches to retrieve the slip of paper for him.

But James was stiff and unyielding, bending carelessly, brushing Domine aside so that she lost her balance and squatted in a heap on the carpet. Immediately he was all contrition, thrusting his papers on one side, and bending down to help her up.

'Leave me alone,' she said, near to tears, this final humiliation achieving what his earlier taunts had not.

'Domine!' he exclaimed entreatingly, 'don't upset yourself like this. God, I only want what's best for you!'

'For you, you mean,' she retorted tightly, turning her head away, and with a stifled groan he knelt beside her on the soft carpet, turning her face to his with a controlled movement.

'Domine,' he muttered, a trifle thickly, 'don't make me hate myself!'

Domine stared at him. 'I thought it was me you hated,' she murmured, in a soft voice.

His eyes darkened, and there was a disturbing light in their depths. 'I don't hate you,' he said, breathing rather heavily. His fingers gripped her wrists, the tips caressing the inner side where a pulse jerked unevenly. Then, as though unable to prevent himself, he bent his mouth to hers, pressing her back against the carpet with the whole weight of his body. Passion flared between them as it had done that day on the moors, and Domine surrendered herself to the searching, demanding compulsion of his kiss. He groaned her name hoarsely, burying his face in her hair, sliding the silk gown from her soft shoulders, and allowing his fingers to caress the length of her body. There was gentleness as well as passion in his touch, and the kisses he pressed on her eyes and cheeks and throat were deep and satisfying, arousing her as his violence had done, but more powerfully, so that she slid her arms round his neck, stroking his ears and his nape, twining her fingers in his thick hair. If the weight of his body pressing her against the carpet was pain, then there was pleasure in it, too, and she had no desire to resist. It wasn't until his urgent hands unbuttoned the bodice of her pyjamas and his mouth sought the gentle curve of her breast that an awful awareness of what she was doing came to her, and even then she couldn't blame him entirely. She had invited this, now she had to repel it if she wanted to maintain her self-respect.

With a sob, she pushed him hard away from her, and the unexpectedness of her rejection caught him unawares. She slid from his arms and ran across the room to the bathroom, unable to quell the sobs that rose in her throat. Entering the bathroom, without a backward glance, she slammed the door and rammed home the bolt with trembling fingers, then leaned back against the door as waves of hot humiliation swept over her. Her breath came in choking gulps and the tightness in her chest had nothing to do with pulmonary causes. Oh, God, she thought wildly. What have I done? What have I done?

There was no sound from the bedroom, and she must have lain there against the door for several minutes before she heard Mrs. Mannering calling her.

'Domine! Domine! Are you in the bathroom?'

Domine swallowed. 'Y – Yes! I'm here!' she managed, her mouth dry.

'Well, hurry up, child. Dr. Rivers is here to see you!'

Domine managed to reply and hastily went to the basin and washed her tear-stained face. Then she rubbed it dry briskly, bringing up a red flush on her cheeks so that the redness of her eyes would be less noticeable. She fastened her gown closely about her, smoothed her hair, and emerged into the bedroom.

'This – this is a late call, doctor,' she managed lightly.

Dr. Rivers smiled. 'I was in the neighbourhood. I've been playing chess with young Morley, and I thought I might call this evening and save myself a job tomorrow. You're looking much better, young woman. I think tomorrow we might let you put on your clothes and get a breath of fresh air, eh?'

Domine nodded and smiled, but inside she was a mass of nerves. The last thing she wanted was to be allowed to go downstairs, to mix with the family again, now that she had destroyed completely all chances of any kind of relationship with James.

But she need not have felt any twinges of anxiety, for when Lily brought her early morning tea the next morning she also brought the news that Mr. James had departed early for London, and was expecting to fly to Rome later in the day.

CHAPTER NINE

DURING the first few days that Domine was back on her feet again Melanie saw to it that the younger girl performed no tiring tasks. Mrs. Mannering seemed indifferent to the girl's weakened condition now that James had gone, and she had Domine running all the little errands she had used to do before. It was Domine who was given the task of taking up Lucia Marcinello's breakfast, but after the first morning that this happened Lucia herself came downstairs for the meal and thus alleviated this chore. Domine spent quite a lot of time outside in the crisp December air, but as Melanie was always around to prevent her from exhausting herself, she spent most of her days exercising the horses or grooming them. Everyone seemed pleased to have her around again and even the two men who worked about the farm came to offer their good wishes.

Lucia spent most of her time in her room, only emerging for meals or occasionally to drive into one of the nearby towns. She had hired a car from a firm in Malton and once or twice she asked Domine to accompany her. But although Domine thanked her warmly, she always refused. Somehow she couldn't bear to spend any time with the woman it seemed likely that James might eventually marry. Although he had said Lucia meant nothing to him his actions on her behalf had belied that statement, and Domine couldn't believe he could prefer Yvonne Park to her. Of course, there was the possibility that someone new might loom on his horizon, but that didn't seem particularly likely, not with Lucia here at Grey Witches.

The days passed slowly. Domine refused to consider what would happen when James returned at Christmas as he surely would. She thought of running away, but she had no money of her own apart from the build-up of a small allowance which Great-Uncle Henry had made her and which had stopped on his death. James Mannering had never got around to discussing allowances, and she had not liked to suggest such a thing when her position was so precarious and involuntary. And without money, there was little she could do. She would have to live while she looked round for a job, and she would have to have somewhere to stay. Lodging houses always wanted cash in advance and she would also need food for perhaps a month before obtaining her first pay cheque in a bank or a library. It was an impossible situation, and there seemed no way of resolving it.

During the second week after James's departure, she was offered an alternative. Vincent had taken her out to a cinema one evening, and on the way home he astounded her by proposing. At first she hadn't taken him seriously, but when she saw his hurt expression as she chided him about it, she realized he was perfectly serious.

'But, Vincent, we've only known one another a little over six weeks,' she exclaimed. 'How can you possibly be sure about something as serious as this?'

Vincent drew up the Land-Rover in the shelter of some tall oaks, and extinguished the vehicle's headlights, turning on the interior light instead. 'I knew almost from the first moment we met,' he exclaimed extravagantly. 'You're so different from the usual run of girls whose only desire is to have a good time. And in a job like mine, that's important.'

Domine sighed, wondering how to let him down

lightly. This was one possibility she had not even thought of.

'But I don't love you, Vincent,' she began gently.

'That will come – with time,' he promised eagerly. 'After all, love is something that grows out of knowing one another, out of living together. I doubt if many couples actually love one another before marriage. Oh, they imagine they do, but that's not real love. Love is being with someone, sharing life with them. Sharing troubles as well as happiness!'

Domine half-smiled. So that was Vincent's definition of love. Well, it was vastly different from her own.

'I think what you're talking about is liking one another,' she murmured unhappily. 'Loving's altogether different. Loving is needing someone so desperately that you wonder how you can live without them! Love is like a fire in the blood that burns you up with its intensity!'

'That's infatuation!' exclaimed Vincent chillingly. 'And how would you know, anyway?' His face darkened. 'Unless – unless you imagine yourself in love with somebody else! Is that it? Is that how you profess to know so much about it?'

Domine coloured. 'Maybe,' she admitted tentatively. 'At any rate, I know I don't love you, and I'm not the one you should marry. Maybe you need someone like Melanie. She has all the attributes I have not, and she likes the life about the estate.'

'Melanie!' Vincent hunched his shoulders. 'Melanie's always wrapped up with her horses. Besides, I don't think Mother would like Melanie.'

Domine shook her head in amusement. There was something so ludicrous about sitting out here, in the grounds of Grey Witches, discussing the merits of who

Vincent ought to marry. With great daring, she said:

'Do you think whether or not your mother approves is so important? I mean – your mother will die one day. Oh, I don't mean to be unkind, but you must live your own life. Not the life your mother would choose for you. And anyway,' she finished, 'I think Melanie's a marvellous person, and she'd make someone a marvellous wife and mother.'

Vincent frowned.'Do you really think so?' he murmured. Then he seemed to pull himself up short. 'But this is ridiculous! I don't want to marry Melanie. I want to marry you. Oh, Domine, please say you will.'

'I'm sorry, Vincent, but I can't.' Domine bent her head.

'So there is someone else.'

'You might say that.'

'Who is it?' Vincent stared at her, and realization seemed to dawn in his eyes. 'You don't – you can't possibly imagine yourself in love with James Mannering!'

Domine's colour deepened. 'Why pick on him?' she asked evasively.

'Because, apart from myself, he's the only personable male around here.'

Domine shrugged. 'It could be someone I knew at the convent.'

Vincent breathed hard down his nose. 'I don't believe it. But this is even more ridiculous! James is thirty-six, almost thirty-seven. He's ten years older than I am!'

'Age has nothing to do with anything,' Domine flared, unable to stand the comparison.

Vincent heaved a sigh. 'You know you're wasting

your time, don't you?' He gave a harsh chuckle. 'Mrs. Mannering has her sights aimed much higher. Haven't you met the illustrious Miss Park?'

'James won't marry her.'

'What makes you so sure?'

'Would you install one woman in your house if you intended to marry another?'

'Oh, I see. You mean Signora Marcinello?'

'Precisely.'

Vincent shrugged. 'It must be nice to be rich and affluent. To be sought after by the world's most beautiful women!' He glanced at Domine wryly. 'So what will you do?'

'At the end of six months Mr. Mannering will enable me to get a job,' she replied quietly. 'Not here. I don't want to stay in the north. I'd prefer to live in the south.' Far away from Grey Witches, she finished silently.

Vincent shrugged again. 'Oh, well, if you're adamant, there's nothing more to be said. But promise me you'll think about it.'

Domine promised, but her eyes were distant. How different two men could be. Vincent had not even kissed her, yet he had asked her to marry him, and James, to whom she had so nearly surrendered, wanted no part of her.

The next morning, she was out with the horses when she encountered the postman in the drive, on his way up to the house. Smiling, she said:

'Can I take the letters for you, Mr. Meridew?'

Alf Meridew scratched his head. 'Surely,' he said, studying the mail in his hands, and then extracting several he handed them to her as she sat astride Rosie. 'Lovely morning! Soon be Christmas. Think it'll be a white one?'

'I hope so,' exclaimed Domine, with enthusiasm.

'Well, I don't,' retorted Alf, with a grin. 'My round's twice as hard when there's snow on the ground – or slush either for that matter.'

Domine smiled at him, and bidding her good morning, he went off on his way, and Domine cantered Rosie back to the stables. As she dismounted, she idly flicked through the letters in her hand. Occasionally Susan wrote to her, but there was none bearing Susan's scrawling handwriting today. However, there was a letter addressed to her, a rather official-looking communication with the name of a firm of solicitors stamped in the top left corner.

Domine stared at this letter in surprise. She had never received any letters from this firm of solicitors before. Certainly, they were not the Leeds-based solicitors who had handled the particulars of her great-uncle's will. This firm was in business in Bognor, and her heart fluttered slightly at the implications.

With a strange desire for secrecy, she stuffed the letter into the pocket of her pants, and leaving Rosie she entered the hall and placed the rest of the letters on the salver resting on the table there. Then, almost guiltily, she ran up the stairs to her room, and closing her door ripped open the envelope.

The paper the letter was written on was the finest vellum and had an expensive feel to it. The contents were brief, and to the point. Domine read the letter once, gave an involuntary gasp, and sinking down on to the bed, she read it again. Even the second time it seemed unreal and unbelievable, and she was trembling when she re-read it a third time. It began:

My dear Miss Grainger,
    It was recently brought to our notice by Mr. Amos

Lancer, owner of Cromptons Hotel, Bognor, that his patron, Mr. Henry Farriday, had not made his usual arrangements for his Christmas vacation there with your good self. His instructions were to inform us if this event ever took place, and as you will realize, our investigations brought us into contact with the firm of Grant, Campbell and Dawson who advised us of your late great-uncle's demise, and subsequent reading of the will they hold. However, it is our duty to inform you that your great-uncle made a second will with us in which you, yourself, are the sole major beneficiary, and as this will is dated later than that held by the said solicitors, Grant, Campbell and Dawson, it can most definitely be held up as the late Henry Farriday's last will and testament.

There were further particulars about dates and information about minor bequests her great-uncle had made to his staff, but the main portion of the letter was what Domine was most interested in. It was an incredible thing to happen, and yet this was possibly just the sort of situation Henry Farriday would have wished. Certainly, it looked as though Mrs. Mannering's suspicions had been justified all along, and that he had indeed avenged the humiliation she had bestowed upon him.

Domine was still sitting there, staring at the letter when Lily called that breakfast was ready and it took a great deal of courage to hide the letter in her suitcase and descend the stairs as though nothing momentous had happened. But during the course of the meal of which she ate little, the whole weight of the problem she was now faced with descended upon her. How could she possibly tell Mrs. Mannering she was no longer the real mistress of Grey Witches? How could she take over the management of an estate of this size when she had no earthly idea how to run it? What perverted streak in her uncle's make-up had caused him to do such a thing?

She poured herself a second cup of coffee and leaning over to Melanie, she said: 'Could you possibly give me a cigarette?'

Melanie looked surprised, but apart from a sardonic quirk of her eyebrows, she said nothing, merely handed over her case that had a lighter combined. Domine lit one, inhaled deeply, and then exhaled with exaggerated effort. Lucia studied her expression thoughtfully, and frowned.

'Surely I have not seen you smoking before?' she exclaimed. 'What has caused this sudden desire for nicotine?'

Domine shrugged, tapping ash unnecessarily. 'No particular reason,' she denied. 'I just felt like one.' Then she smiled to take the sharpness out of her reply.

Mrs. Mannering eyed her strangely. 'Is something troubling you, Domine?' she queried, with resignation. 'You're not sickening for anything again, are you?'

Melanie grimaced in her aunt's direction. 'Such concern!' she commented dryly. 'What's the matter, Aunt Geraldine? Can you feel another headache coming on?'

Domine rose abruptly from the table, and left the room. She felt she couldn't bear their bickering this morning. She needed to talk about this to somebody, but to whom? Who could she confide in? Certainly not Mrs. Mannering, or Melanie either for that matter. Vincent? She frowned. Not after his proposal last evening. Somehow that had alienated their relationship. She sighed. Why was it always sex that caused rifts in people's lives?

That left only one person – Lucia Marcinello.

Domine sighed. She was loath to put any form of ammunition into the Italian woman's hands, and yet possibly she was the only person who could listen objectively.

With sudden decision, she returned to the door of the dining-room, and supporting herself against the lintel, she said: 'Signora Marcinello! Could – could I see you for a moment?'

The surprise on Mrs. Mannering's and Melanie's faces was almost comical, but Lucia Marcinello did not demur. She merely nodded, pushed back her chair, and came out into the hall where Domine waited nervously.

'Yes?' she said curiously, 'what is it?'

Domine bit her lip. 'We can't talk here. Could – could we take your car and go for a drive?'

Lucia frowned. 'If you like,' she agreed. 'But I must put on some shoes,' she indicated the elegant fur-lined mules she was wearing.

Domine nodded. 'All right, I'll get my coat.'

She followed Lucia up the stairs, and speeding along to her room she collected the letter as well as her red overcoat. Then, wrapping the coat closely about her, she descended the stairs again to join Lucia.

Once in the car, she relaxed a little. It was a beautiful morning, the mist just rising from the moors, and the promise of a crisp day ahead. Smoke hung sleepily in the atmosphere, and there was the pungent scent of dampness and bonfires, and rotting vegetation. Country smells that Domine had grown to appreciate.

Lucia asked no questions until they were about a mile from Grey Witches, on the moorland road, on a

sweep of land from where the sea was visible. Lucia
parked the car, offered Domine a cigarette, and after
they were lit said:

'Now what is troubling you? Is it James?'

Domine glanced at her sharply. 'Why do you say
that?'

Lucia gave her a speculative look. 'You ask me that!'
she countered. 'Obviously something happened between you and James the night before he left for
Italy.'

Domine flushed. 'Did he tell you?'

Lucia shook her head. 'Oh, no. James is not a man
to bring his troubles to anyone, least of all a woman,
but I know him quite well now, and I know when he is
disturbed. And he was disturbed before he left, and
that was why he left, wasn't it?'

Domine sighed. 'Oh, I suppose so. Though why I
should tell you amazes me.'

Lucia looked puzzled. 'Why? Surely of all the people
here I am the least involved, and therefore the easiest
to tell.'

Domine looked steadily at her. 'Do you love James?'
she asked daringly.

Lucia uttered a gasp. 'Love James?' she echoed. 'No,
of course I do not love him, and certainly he does not
love me, if that is to be your next question.'

'But—' Domine broke off. 'You are so – so close!'

'Of course. We are good friends. I have told you – he
and Giulio were friends. They had known one another
for many years. It was natural that James and I should
get to know one another. But it is not an intimate relationship.' Lucia sighed now. 'Sometimes – only sometimes – I wish James would see me as a woman, and
not as Giulio's wife, but—' she shrugged. 'He is not
interested in me. There – now – what is all this secrecy

176

about? Why this urgent need for privacy? What has happened? Are you pregnant or something?'

'No!' Domine was horrified. 'Of course not.'

Lucia shrugged in a continental fashion. 'Why "of course not"?' she parried. 'You mean James has never made love to you?'

'No!' Domine stared at her aghast.

Lucia gave an exclamation. 'I begin to understand his disturbance,' she murmured, rather sardonically. Then she pressed Domine's arm. 'Do not look so distraught, Domine. You cannot look me in the eyes and tell me he would not like to do so!'

Domine pressed the palms of her hands to her cheeks. 'How do you know all this?'

Lucia spread her hands. 'I am Italian,' she said, as though that explained everything. 'When he bought you the gown, I felt certain—'

'The *gown*!' echoed Domine. 'You mean – the gown you gave me?'

'But of course.' Lucia sighed. 'Ah, you are very naïve, little Domine. And James read you correctly. He said you would not have taken it from him. That was why he asked me to give you it.'

Domine stared down at her hands clasped in her lap. 'I see,' she murmured, almost inaudibly, remembering with clarity the way she had taunted him when he had not expressed admiration of the dressing gown. An awful sense of embarrassment swept over her, but Lucia brushed it aside as she said: 'Well? Are you going to tell me, or are you not?'

Domine swallowed hard, and then fumbling in her pocket she brought out the letter and handed it wordlessly to Lucia. Lucia drew it out of its envelope and read it silently. Then she whistled softly through her teeth, and a small chuckle escaped her. 'So?' she said, with amusement. 'The mistress of Grey Witches is no mistress at all. Poor Geraldine! She will be most upset!'

Domine compressed her lips. Then she said slowly: 'The point is, I don't want it – not any of it! James was his son. He is entitled to everything, not me! My uncle only used me, can't you see that? His reasons for taking me away from the orphanage – they have meaning now. He needed a scapegoat, and I'm it!'

'Oh, now, Domine, you are hardly the scapegoat!' Lucia shook her head. 'On the contrary, of all of them, you have come out of this best. You are now a wealthy young woman. And as far as one can understand, there's absolutely no reason why you shouldn't sell Grey Witches and the estate, and live on the capital until you find yourself some nice wealthy boy-friend!'

'No!' Domine was adamant. 'I don't want his house, or his estate, or his money! I think he behaved abominably in his life, and even more abominably at his death! He must have known that unless by some quirk of fate he happened to die during the three months of the year we spent at Bognor, the earlier will would be produced and acted upon. I'm convinced that's why he left those instructions with Mr. Lancer. He hoped this would happen. He hoped the second will wasn't found until Mrs. Mannering, and James, had actually become beneficiaries in every sense of the word.'

'You may be right,' Lucia conceded, 'but nevertheless, this will has been found and the Mannerings will have to know about it.'

'No!' Domine buried her face in her hands. 'Oh, Signora Marcinello, I don't want that to happen. Oh, what can I do?' There was despair in her voice, and Lucia felt a sense of responsibility assail her suddenly.

'These solicitors,' she consulted the letter, 'Hayman, Brown and Partners of Bognor. Why don't you go to see them? Tell them how you feel. See if you can't work something out between you.'

'Such as what? I don't want to be the beneficiary. I mean that.'

Lucia frowned. 'Nevertheless, you have expressed some doubts about your future, and it might be a good idea if you retained sufficient of the capital to enable you to find somewhere to live, wherever you want to live, and to bank something for your English rainy day.'

Domine saw the logic of this, and she nodded slowly. 'I suppose I could do that. I had half expected Great-Uncle Henry would leave me something to exist on until I found a job of sorts. I don't anticipate any difficulties in that direction really. My qualifications are reasonable.'

'All right, then. All you have to do is to get down to Bognor and see these solicitors as soon as possible. There are trains, are there not? You could go today – this afternoon.'

Domine hesitated. 'But what about Mrs. Mannering? And Melanie? What can I tell them?'

'Tell them nothing,' advised Lucia thoughtfully. 'Look, if you like, I can drive you to the station this afternoon. We can find out the times of trains and so on, but no one need know you have left until you are gone. That way you avoid explanations, and I will assure them that you are in good hands. Then, when you come back, everything will be settled, and you will not feel this sense of inadequacy or apprehension at facing the formidable Mrs. Mannering.'

'Oh, Lucia!' Domine clasped her hands. 'That

sounds a wonderful idea.' Then she coloured. 'I mean –
Signora—'

'Lucia will do,' remarked the Italian woman dryly.
'So! We have no time to waste. Already we are arousing suspicion by being out here alone. Come! We
will go back and think of some excuse for driving out
again this afternoon.'

As the car turned back towards Grey Witches,
Domine said, thoughtfully: 'I could offer to show you
the historical monuments of York!'

'So you could,' agreed Lucia. 'Particularly the rail-
way station!'

Crompton's Hotel was exactly as Domine remembered it to be and she couldn't suppress a faint shudder
as she mounted the steps and entered the lobby. It was
three days since she had left Yorkshire and during that
time she had accomplished much of what she had intended.

The solicitors, Hayman, Brown and Partners, had
been very kind and very helpful, understanding the
terrible position she was faced with. Mr. Brown himself
had handled the will from its inception and he it was
who advised her to think very carefully before com-
mitting herself to actions she might later regret.

'You tell me this son of the late Mr. Farriday is the
playwright, James Mannering,' he said. 'Surely, therefore, he is not without funds in his own right?'

Domine sighed. 'It's not the money,' she tried to
explain. 'It's the house, Grey Witches. It should belong
to James. His mother is already its mistress. I couldn't
destroy that!'

Mr. Brown tugged at his chin thoughtfully. 'Nevertheless, your great-uncle left everything to you. You
have explained about the rather unusual aspects of this

situation, but while I accept that Mr. Mannering is possibly the natural heir, Mr. Farriday did in fact change his will in your favour, and I would advise you to consider what your position will be if you reject everything.'

Domine sighed again. 'But don't you see, my great-uncle only used me as a kind of whipping boy.' She pressed her finger tips to her temples. 'Oh, that's not exactly what I mean. It's difficult to explain, but surely you can see that this was his way of avenging himself against Mrs. Mannering for refusing his offer of marriage.'

Mr. Brown lit a cigar with deliberation. 'Aren't you dramatizing the facts, somewhat?' he queried gently. 'Very few people would carry a grudge to their grave.'

Domine looked at him seriously. 'And can you say in all honesty that my great-uncle was incapable of doing just that?'

Mr. Brown moved uncomfortably. 'No, I suppose not,' he agreed slowly. 'The fact that your uncle made two wills with different solicitors points to his desiring to create some kind of disturbance at his death. But even so, have you thought what this means to you in terms of money—'

'I'm not interested in the money,' cried Domine impatiently. 'I know I need a little, sufficient at least to enable me to find somewhere to live and to keep me until I'm earning an adequate income, but apart from that I want nothing. I want you to contact Grant, Campbell and Dawson before they have time to do anything about this and explain that the terms of the old will are going to stand in almost every aspect.'

Mr. Brown studied the tip of his cigar. 'Very well, Miss Grainger, if this is really what you want.' He gave a slight smile. 'It seems your uncle made one mistake anyway. He should have inserted a clause preventing you from doing exactly what you are doing if he had wanted to make it completely watertight.'

Domine considered this. 'I think my great-uncle made several errors of judgement,' she conceded. 'I suppose he imagined James would either abandon me completely, or at best leave me in the convent until I was eighteen. Had that happened, I suppose it was just conceivable that not knowing James and his mother and the circumstances surrounding their presence at Grey Witches, I might have accepted the terms of this second will without question. At any rate, he obviously believed his son had as little humanity as he seems to have had.' Her voice broke, suddenly.

Mr. Brown nodded his head understandingly. 'Very well, Miss Grainger. We'll act on your instructions. I'll be in touch with you in a day or two to finalize the details. Is there somewhere you can stay?'

'I've booked in at a hotel,' Domine nodded.

'Crompton's Hotel?'

Domine shook her head vigorously. 'No,' she said firmly, 'not Crompton's Hotel.'

But that was two days ago now, and this morning Domine had signed away her inheritance, but some strange sense of curiosity had drawn her here, to Crompton's Hotel, to see it for the last time. It was late afternoon, and there was a tea lounge where one could have afternoon tea. She knew the tea lounge very well, very well indeed, she thought reflectively. How many hours had she sat in there with Great-uncle Henry, watching him play interminable games of chess with an elderly retired colonel from one of the colonial regiments? That was exactly the kind of hotel it was, she realized now with her new insight into human relationships. It was the kind of hotel where school-mistresses went to retire, or colonels, or men who wished to escape from the realities of their life, she thought with distaste.

The receptionist didn't recognize her, and she made her way into the tea lounge, taking a table near the window which looked out on the promenade. There were a few couples taking the air, but a sea mist had banished all but the most hardy. In the summer, the promenade was thronged with people, and there were lots of children. But in the winter the seaside was for old people, not the young.

The waitress who came to take her order eyed her strangely, then blinked rapidly. 'It's Miss Grainger, isn't it?' she exclaimed, in astonishment. 'Why, fancy you being here, taking tea! I thought as how your uncle was dead.' She flushed. 'Begging your pardon, miss!'

'Mr. Farriday is dead,' said Domine, without emotion. 'I'm just here on a visit, Josie. Er – could I have some tea – and some cigarettes!'

Josie's mouth tilted. 'You – smoking, miss?' she exclaimed. 'Well, fancy that. Do you want cakes, too?'

'No, thank you. Just tea.' Domine managed a slight smile and watched the portly figure of Josie as she made her way across the almost deserted restaurant to the swing doors into the kitchen.

But as Josie disappeared, a man came into the restaurant and stood looking around broodingly until his eyes lighted on Domine. Then he strode purposefully through the tables to her side, and staring down at her with angry eyes, he exclaimed: 'For God's sake, Domine, I've searched everywhere for you! What in hell are you doing here?'

Domine quivered. 'I might ask you the same thing,

Mr. Mannering,' she said unsteadily. 'I – I'm having tea. Won't you join me?'

'No, I won't. And you're coming with me. I want to talk to you, and what I have to say can't be said in this miserable place!'

Domine shivered. 'I don't think we have anything to say to one another that can't be said here,' she retorted, with an amazing amount of calm, considering she was a quaking mass inside.

James's eyes darkened. 'Do you want me to pick you up and carry you bodily out of here?' he muttered savagely, 'because by God, I'll do it if I have to!'

Domine got uncertainly to her feet. 'You – you wouldn't dare,' she gasped.

'Try me!' he urged her fiercely.

She glanced round. The few tables that were occupied were viewing their confrontation with some interest, and with an angry glance in his direction she swept across the room to the door. As she reached it, Josie emerged from the kitchen with her tray.

'Why, Miss Grainger, you're not leaving!' she exclaimed in surprise.

'Miss Grainger is,' said James precisely. 'If you wish to charge for your trouble, send the bill to Mr. Farriday's solicitors. Mr. Lancer knows their address.'

'Y-yes, sir.' Josie was obviously astounded, and Domine, her cheeks burning, made her way outside.

But once there she turned on James furiously. 'All right,' she said, 'you've got your way. I've left the restaurant. But now you can't make me go with you.'

'Can't I?' He gave a wry smile, and bent to open the door of the sleek sports car parked at the kerb. 'Get in.'

'But this is a restricted parking area,' she began.

'You're not allowed to park here!'

'I don't intend to,' he snapped. 'Get in!'

Unwillingly Domine acquiesced. There was a sense of defeat about her, and she hadn't the strength for much more fighting.

James slid in beside her, his thigh brushing hers, and then turning on the ignition, he put the car smoothly into gear. They shot away down the promenade and Domine felt somehow that this was inevitable. She didn't know how or why he was here, but there was nothing she could do about it now.

He drove out of the town and parked on the cliffs some distance from the road. Then he turned in his seat and said harshly: 'You're a crazy idiot, do you know that?'

Domine heaved a sigh. 'In what particular connection are you meaning?' she inquired wearily. 'I seem to have done nothing but crazy things ever since I left the convent!'

James gave her a long considering look. 'I mean – Henry's will,' he replied quietly. 'And you know it.'

Domine shrugged. 'How do you know about that?'

James gave a brief ejaculation. 'Surely you must have realized that Grant, Campbell and Dawson were bound to contact me in the circumstances, as the chief beneficiary in the old will?'

'But you were in Italy!' she exclaimed.

'No, I was not. I returned a few days ago.'

'You didn't contact your mother.'

'No, I needed time to think,' he muttered, rather huskily. 'And I could hardly come back, could I? After what happened.'

Domine's cheeks burned. 'It's your home.'

'Correction. It's yours.'

'Not any more. I signed it over to you this morning.'

James gave her a sardonic smile. 'You're still under age, remember? It needs verification. I refused to give it.'

Domine stared at him. 'You've seen Mr. Brown?'

'This afternoon,' he agreed quietly. 'We had a long discussion about you.'

'Oh, James!' She pressed her hands to her cheeks. 'I don't want the house or the money! It's what your mother said all along. Henry's reasons for getting me out of the orphanage were all selfish ones!'

James slid an arm around her, but gently, without passion. 'Oh, Domine,' he murmured softly, 'you're so ready to think the worst of yourself, aren't you? Has it never occurred to you that Henry might have taken such a liking to you that he wanted you to have his possessions? That he wanted you to be the mistress of Grey Witches?'

Domine bent her head. 'Why should he do that? I'm such an ordinary person. He had no reason to care about me.'

'That's nonsense, and you know it,' muttered James roughly. 'You're sweet, and you're gentle, and you can be quite formidable when you choose!' He smiled. 'And you're intelligent, and a man can talk to you! Why shouldn't my father have loved you? I do.'

Domine's heart skipped a beat and she looked at him disbelievingly. Then she hunched her shoulders and shook her head. 'Oh, stop trying to be nice to me!' she exclaimed miserably. 'I don't want your – your – pity!'

James's arm tightened about her, drawing her close against the hard strength of his body. Taking her hand, he placed it against his chest and said, rather thickly:

'Can you feel that – that unsteady beat? Does that feel like pity?' One hand cupped her throat. 'You're adorable, Domine,' he murmured unsteadily, 'and after the torment you've put me through these last couple of weeks thinking I'd destroyed any chance we had of happiness together by my clumsiness, I can't be expected to feel pity for anyone but myself.' He put his mouth against hers gently, but as her lips parted his mouth hardened, and he had to wrench himself away at last. 'This isn't the place for this,' he groaned huskily. 'And anyway, we have some things to settle first.'

Domine's whole being was seething with happiness. Cupping his face in her hands, she traced the outline of his mouth with her fingers until he turned his lips to her palm, pressing her hand against his mouth for a moment. 'Domine,' he muttered, putting her away from him, 'I'm trying to be sensible. Don't make me want you any more than I do already. I'm only human!'

Domine folded her hands demurely and looked at him through her lashes. 'Go on,' she said softly. 'I'll be good – for a while.'

James smiled, and fumbling in his pocket brought out his cigarettes. After one was lit and he had inhaled deeply, he said: 'First of all, I want you to keep Grey Witches.'

Domine's face changed. 'Why?'

James sighed. 'Honey, legally it's yours anyway until you're eighteen in a couple of months' time. But eighteen is not a very great age, and I don't want you to leave Grey Witches and get some place of your own where it might be difficult for me to be with you—'

Domine frowned. 'But – but what do you mean?' Her voice quivered.

187

James heaved a sigh. 'Oh, Domine, please don't make it any harder for me than it already is. I know what you're thinking – what you're imagining – but it's not like that. I want you, I need you, I don't deny that, but you're too young yet to be certain that it's me you want! Can you see that? I can't run the risk of destroying your life. What I have I hold, and once we were married I'd never be able to let you go!'

'So – so what is your suggestion?' she asked tautly. 'I – I presume you have one.'

James raked a hand through his hair. 'We wait – say until you're twenty. I'll be thirty-nine then. The gap won't seem so insurmountable!'

Domine shivered. 'And if I refuse?'

James drew deeply on his cigarette, rather jerkily. 'That's your prerogative, of course,' he said shortly.

Domine stared at him. How could she make this stubborn man see that she was not like other girls? She didn't care about the things they cared about. She didn't want entertainment, excitement – teenage things. Entertainment for her meant riding across the wild expanses of the moor; excitement was being in the presence of the man she loved.

Wanting to hurt him as he was hurting her, she said: 'Vincent Morley asked me to marry him. I told him I'd think it over.'

James did not speak, but continued to smoke his cigarette, staring bleakly out across the cliffs to the sea beyond. Domine watched him loving the curve of his jawline, the thick darkness of his hair, the brilliance of his eyes. She loved everything about this man with an intensity that amounted to pain. Didn't he know? Couldn't he feel her love?

'Did you hear what I said?' she asked tightly.

He turned his eyes in her direction and she saw the

gauntness of his face. 'I heard,' he said grimly. 'And have you?'

'What?'

'Thought it over,' he snapped savagely.

'Yes,' she whispered. Then her fit of aggression left her. 'I'm sorry, James, I'm sorry.'

Her submission aroused him as her aggressiveness never could, and with a stifled exclamation he pulled her back into his arms, burying his face in her neck. 'I didn't believe you could care for me,' he muttered achingly, 'not after the way I'd treated you, and then Lucia told me about your conversation with her and I gambled that she was right.'

'You've spoken to Lucia?' exclaimed Domine. 'When?'

'On the telephone, yesterday. She told me I'd be a fool to let the difference in our ages matter.' He drew back to look at her. 'But I haven't the right to take away your youth—'

'If you go away, you'll take away my life,' she murmured, against his chest. 'James, please don't make us wait. All right, until I'm eighteen I won't press you, but if I'm old enough to vote surely I'm old enough to decide what I want out of life!'

James tipped her face up to his. 'You do have a point,' he murmured huskily. 'But I warn you, it may not be easy. I'm used to living alone, and I'm a brute when I'm writing and it isn't going well. I shall probably spend hours alone in my study and then come out and bully you—'

'And then we'll make love,' finished Domine, drawing his mouth to hers.

James rested his forehead against hers. 'How can I refuse when I want you so much?' he muttered a trifle roughly. 'I think I began wanting you that very first

189

day when I brought you back to the apartment. You were such an aggressive little thing. I wanted to protect you, and then later I realized I had to protect you from myself. I think that was when I began despising myself. But God forgive me, I love you so much, I can't let you go.'

Domine stroked his cheek. 'Well, at least your mother can keep Grey Witches,' she said gently. 'And Melanie can keep the stables. And when we have children they'll be able to learn to ride there and love the moors as I do—'

'Steady on,' murmured James, with his mouth against hers. 'I shall want you to myself for quite some time yet . . .'